FAT VAMPIRE 6

FAT VAMPIRE 6

FAT VAMPIRE 6

Survival of the Fattest

JOHNNY B TRUANT

For all the fat vampires out there.

ONE

Dark City
_____

FORTY YEARS LATER

REGINALD PULLED his car into the garage and killed the engine. The video screens on the windshields and windows all flickered off, turning the car's interior into a black pod. He opened the car door in the light-sealed garage, throwing it wide without checking first to make sure that the room was closed. The car knew its dock; its sensors wouldn't allow the door to open if there was any sunlight in the room. But Reginald wasn't trusting the technology. It was more that even after four decades spent undead, he'd never quite gotten used to not being human.

He closed the car door behind him, then crossed the garage to the door that led into the house. He left his shoes in the mud room and walked up into the large kitchen. The place's marble and chrome surfaces sparkled. The service had been in while he'd been at work, and the smell of lemon-scented chemicals still hung in the air. Reginald wrinkled his nose. He didn't like the smell, and he didn't like having other people in his house. He also didn't like the company's rate structure. Who charged by the minute? But that, again, was human thinking. Reginald had once hired a cleaning service in Ohio, and the human maids had taken hours to do their jobs. The vampire cleaners, on the other hand, could do their work during a TV commercial break. But despite his protests, Nikki had insisted. "I'm not a maid," she told him. "I'm a sex slave."

Reginald put his satchel down on the kitchen island, knowing that Nikki would yell at him about it as she always did. But the way Reginald saw it, the kitchen might as well be a dumping ground. They could put their financial records in the oven. They could fill the pantry with linens. And yes, they could use the island to drop off their bags and keys. Why wouldn't they? They were vampires, and they didn't need a kitchen. That was the thinking that had gone into the first wave of homes built after Turnover, anyway — houses built with only a nook for a blood refrigerator and a microwave. But today those houses were hard to sell, and new construction had re-learned what humans had always known: that kitchens and bathrooms were what sold houses. It was as if Turnover had been a U-turn in the stream of time rather than a point on a line. Humanity had progressed forward, and then vampires had taken over the planet and bounced back in the same direction. More and more vampires cooked these days, and big kitchens were once again all the rage. The food magazines and TV shows were back. And as had been the case with human cuisine, the food almost never contained blood.

Reginald walked into the large formal dining room they'd furnished but never used, then into the three-story living room. The house was quiet. Nikki had had a meeting of her super-secret group last night (they pretended to be a human-rights underground, but it was hard to raise indignation these days and Reginald suspected that they were really just lobbyists) and was asleep. Reginald, on the other hand, had been working days lately, trying to get ahead on a new product line. It bothered him to work a schedule that was opposite Nikki's, but the reversion was only temporary. Besides, it seemed as if everyone he employed was working well past dawn lately, and he wasn't even requiring them to do it. Whenever he looked at the clock and found himself bothered by his unnatural schedule, he could just pretend that PM was AM and that AM was PM, and the fullness of the office would make the idea seem legit. With his light-tight car, the company's light-tight parking garage, and the windowless building, it wasn't even a difficult mental trick to pull off.

He strolled back into the kitchen, hungry. He pulled a blood pouch from the refrigerator and drank it cold. Nikki always warmed hers, but Reginald had long ago stopped bothering. Blood was nourishment, nothing more. Drinking it was like taking a vitamin. There were plenty of fancy bloods out there — brands flavored with cinnamon or vanilla, brands infused 50/50 with fruit juice to cut the taste — but Reginald drank his straight. When your food tasted like a cinnamon bun, it was easy to forget that it had been drained from the arm of a man or woman strapped to a table against their will. And if Reginald needed to drink the stuff and be part of the problem, he at least wanted to remind himself where it had come from, and what it had truly cost.

He looked at the empty blood pouch, which he'd bought at a ritzy Top Fang supermarket for twice the price of bargain blood. The label promised that the humans the company bled were free-range. It also claimed that the blood in the pouch contained 33 percent more iron than competing brands. Reginald tossed it into the garbage can.

He turned back to his satchel, then began unpacking its contents in what could have been a flashback from half a century ago: Oreo clones, Ritz cracker clones, Chips Ahoy clones. Nabisco hadn't survived Turnover, the same as most human companies (other than, ironically, Microsoft and Apple — who despite collaborating to develop blood-interfacing AI still didn't get along), but their factories had. Once the human population had been killed, collected, or driven off to hide in their holes outside the vampire cities, the world had become a vast playground — at the time, a playground filled with relics that nobody wanted. *This is a vampire planet now*, pundits had said. *What do vampires need with snack factories and manufacturing plants?*

The answer, of course, turned out to be *plenty*. Reginald could have predicted it, and did. It had been perhaps his last true strategic exercise — the last time he'd held all of the world in his mind and mapped out the inevitable future. As the Vampire Nation tried to make itself comfortable topside, struggling to step into the decimated human economy and use their money, Reginald had scavenged as many old dollars (which held value for a good two years, though they inflated out of control until NewDollars were minted) as he could and had taken the best investment advice a man could receive: to buy what he knew and loved. He'd gotten the old snack factories up and running, harvesting the old companies' recipes and repackaging them under his own brand name, "Snaco." Then he'd waited. And waited. And waited. It took three years before the vampire palate became bored enough to forget that it was only supposed to drink blood, and after that he'd become rich.

Ironically, by the time Reginald's snack factories hit

paydirt, he'd already been cured of his own addiction. The snacks on the counter were lot samples, not household staples. He'd lost his taste for human food when he'd seen how easy it was for a nation of bloodsuckers to forget who and what they were — and, most importantly, what they'd done. From the moment the handwriting proclaiming human defeat had appeared on the wall forty years earlier, Reginald had vowed to never let himself do the same.

Forty years.

He was standing opposite the wall calendar, and he looked at it for a solid fifteen seconds to assure himself that it had really been that long. It was hard to believe. The face he saw in the bathroom mirror today was exactly the same as it had been on the day Reginald's clock had stopped. The same was true of Nikki, of Brian, and of almost everyone else he knew. Only Claire had changed, and it's not like she'd changed in the way anyone had expected, either.

Forty years gone, and still Reginald hadn't finished putting the vampire codex together in his mind. The main reason was that he'd stopped caring when the codex's first earth-shattering prediction had turned out to be bullshit. Then, once he'd stopped caring, it had been simple to stop even trying. He *hated* the codex. Its unsolved, pointless complexity mocked him in the way the treadmills at his human workplace used to mock him. Every day when he closed his eyes to sleep, he saw the codex's partially assembled carcass in his head. It felt like failure — like a home gym purchased with good intentions and then used as a clothes rack. He didn't want to touch the goddamn thing. It reminded him of the seven billion humans who'd died when he'd failed to find or assemble it in time. It reminded him of Maurice, who the codex suggested had sacrificed himself in order to give Reginald the ability to solve the codex — Maurice, who'd died for nothing and who Reginald still dreamed of more often than seemed normal.

The all-knowing *codex*. The precious vampire *codex*. The stupid, motherfucking, cocksucking, dirty asshole of a cunt *codex*.

He didn't need to solve the damn thing anyway. He'd never needed to even look for it, let alone solve it. The codex, to Reginald, had meant nothing but lies and grief. He'd gone around the world to find it, Maurice had died to protect it, and then when Reginald had finally opened its resting place, he'd found that it had been within him all along. What had been the point of the search, other than to make room for more grief and death? And after all of that — after Reginald had figured out the riddle and located the codex right there in his own blood — its dire warning about a human uprising had never even come true. And how *could* it come true? Humans were endangered, and most of those that still existed lived in controlled blood farms, guarded day and night. If that didn't prove that it had all been bullshit, he didn't know what did.

It all felt like a cosmic joke: *Har-har, let's make Reginald dance and laugh when he falls down.* It was the story of his life. Like vampire bodies, nothing ever really changed.

After Turnover, Reginald had again found himself part of a small out-group, not at all a member of the majority. The vampire population had only lost around twenty thousand in the war, which meant that Reginald was one of only fifty thousand vampires alive who'd been turned before the official end of hostilities — marked by the day President Timken had appeared on VNN standing in front of a huge sign declaring MISSION ACCOMPLISHED. At that time there were still millions upon millions of humans still around, and the balance was still skewed. The final human population reduction (that's what they called it; it wasn't an "extermination" in any of the official channels) had taken most of the next year, and during that time, to tip the other side of the scales, vouchers had been given to responsible vampires to begin creating new citizens. The vampire population target was five million, and that number was reached within six months. The spike in growth meant that 99 out of every 100 vampires now in existence had begun their undead lives on a planet ruled by the undead: they'd never been trained as vampires; they'd always gotten their blood from pouches; they hadn't ever needed to hide in the shadows and hunt. These were people who used to be human and who'd remained essentially the same after turning, save their higher velocities and higher sex drives. And at the same time, official troops had eliminated all but five million of the remaining humans, bringing the planet's population balance to 50/50. Ten million living beings on a planet that had once housed seven billion left a lot of empty space, and there was a lot of room to grow. So slowly, as resources allowed, the idea going forward was that the human population would be allowed to grow, and then the best among them would be turned to maintain the balance.

It was a good plan, and after four decades, it seemed to be working. The Vampire Nation had gone on just fine. The angels hadn't shown up with praise or condemnation, and vampires (especially those 99% of new ones) were already beginning to doubt that they'd ever really existed. Reginald had raised a stink when he'd first been duped by the codex (feeling like Jor-El, futilely telling Krypton that the planet was doomed before sending baby Superman into space in a giant sea urchin), but it turned out that nobody wanted to hear about a human war so soon after the last one. Reconstruction required everyone's full attention. There was work to do. Bills to be paid. TV to watch. The irony was that vampires had started the war feeling like humanity had grown soft… but seeing as most modern vampires had never hunted and there were now six dozen vampire cable TV channels, it seemed to Reginald that all the world had done was to swap "soft" for "soft with pointy teeth."

Just as Reginald was starting to wonder if he should head upstairs and slip into bed with Nikki, the phone in his pocket trilled. He pulled it out and looked at it. Then, with a welcome and unexpected smile on his face, he tapped the screen and took the call.

"Hey Claire," he said.

"Hey Reginald," she replied. Then there was a long pause. It was so like Claire. She had something to say, and she'd called him, but now that they were talking she wasn't going to say a thing.

"What's up, Claire?" he said.

On the other end of the line, he heard her swallow. "It's starting," she said.

TWO

Old Young Girl

Claire lived alone on the other side of the city. It broke Reginald's heart that she lived alone, but she said she wanted it that way. What was she supposed to do — shack up with a vampire and have some vampire kids? Because that was all the rage these days, similar to how first-world humans used to adopt children from third-world nations. A well-to-do vampire couple would head to one of the farms, choose a human (usually an adult; kid vampires were creepy), buy them, and then turn them. It was usually illegal to turn humans because enough turnings could skew the balance between the species, but people rich enough to afford their own milker could usually wrangle the necessary connections. The proud parents would then treat the new vampire like a child for the first few weeks, but given that the new vampire was an adult, the relationships usually degraded into three-way marriages. It was a distinct difference versus the old adoption systems.

Reginald, who didn't change from year to year, never got fully used to the fact that Claire did. He somehow expected her to be perpetually ten or eleven as she'd been when he'd met her, when she'd saved the world the first time, and when their joint predictions had failed to save the world the second time. But when he arrived at Claire's door shortly after nightfall that evening, she came to the door as the same grown woman she'd been the last time he'd seen her: petite with long, light brown hair, by all appearances in her late twenties despite actually being 51. Claire considered her inexplicable slow aging to be a happy medium: she wanted to get older, but didn't want to do so quickly. The slowness of it gave Reginald hope. Maybe, if she moved to the outskirts and peeked under enough rocks, she'd be able to find a nice human man while she was still young enough to have a normal life and family with him. Not that "normal" had much meaning in Claire's life.

Reginald said hello. Claire invited him inside. The exchange had an automatic feel, because Claire invited *everyone* inside. She had to. If a courier tried to hand her a package uninvited, he might feel the repellant force that protected her human home against vampires, and that would be bad. But with that small issue aside, she could easily pass for vampire. Thanks to the strange biology she'd exhibited since puberty (something Reginald suspected was due to her father being an ice-penised incubus), Claire registered as cold on the City Protection Corps satellites that watched the city. Her aging was slow enough that her neighbors, who she avoided, hadn't noticed her glacial progression. In another forty years, she might become different enough to make moving a necessity, but for now she was just another vampire next door.

"How do you feel?" Reginald asked, coming inside and making himself comfortable on Claire's couch.

Claire sat on the ottoman across from him. "Okay, I guess. But it's... I don't know how to describe it other than to say that I can feel something starting to… starting to *change*."

"Like you're getting sick again? Like the first time, after the war?"

She shook her head. "Not like that. Something weird was 'waking up' when it started — when I got so sick. I feel it all the time these days, but now it's becoming different. I feel something being wound up. It's changing. It's *starting.*"

"What does that mean?"

Claire flapped her arms, giving a very adolescent expression of frustration. Reginald watched her with pity. In many ways, she'd never had a chance to grow up. There simply hadn't been the time.

"I don't know, Reginald! I *never* know, okay? Same as it's always been. You used to ask me to predict things, but I could never see the information in my head in the way you wanted me to see it. I see everything, every day, as liquid. Things happen and I realize afterward that I'd known they were going to happen all along. I'll go to an appointment early by mistake, realize I've shown up at the wrong time, and then learn that someone wrote the appointment down wrong and that the time I arrived is actually correct. I'll remember that someone promised me something, get angry when they don't remember promising it to me, then realize that I'm recalling a promise made three hundred years ago as if it were yesterday — or, in a few cases, tomorrow. Do you know what that's like? To know everything but not really *know* that you know it, or how to control it?"

Reginald thought of the codex. "Yes," he said.

"It's not like that. I'm not a vampire. You can *see* the information, at least — like it's in a big jumbled filing cabinet. Not me. For me, it's like soup. *You* have control over whether you think about the stuff in your head. I don't.

And so when I call you and tell you that it's starting, *I don't even know what that means. What's* starting? How do I know? Where will it start — whatever 'it' is? Why? Or is it even a real thing?" She began to wipe furiously at her eyes, angry at her own sudden tears of frustration.

"It's okay, Claire. If anyone understands what you feel — how you *live*, I mean — I... well, I'm the closest you've got, I guess."

She rolled her eyes angrily. "I just wish we knew why I am how I am. Have I found the fountain of youth? Or am I just a freak? What am I, Reginald? Am I human? Am I an incubus? Am I a stilted vampire? If we could just get someone to look at my blood..."

Reginald shook his head. They'd been having this argument forever, but there was no way they could take Claire's blood in for analysis. Reginald wanted to understand why she presented as a kind of half-vampire — why she was cold but didn't burn in the sun, why her cuts healed quickly and why she could bend energy and electricity to her will — but it wasn't worth the risk. He had no idea what her blood might reveal, but he knew that unlike himself, Claire didn't require regular infusions of red blood cells to live. For now, nobody was suspicious of her; Claire was cold and dark, stayed indoors, and got regular blood deliveries like everyone else. But if a lab decided that she — or even an anonymous test subject that Reginald somehow had access to — might be human? Well, that would be bad. *Very* bad.

"It's too risky, Claire."

"Couldn't you send it to the people Nikki knows? Those Underground people?"

"You mean the picketers with vague ambitions to one day circulate a petition?"

"Underground science labs. 'Fighting the power' and

whatnot. Those kinds of people must have *a few* nerds with microscopes who could…"

"I told you," Reginald interrupted, "I've looked at your blood under a microscope and it doesn't reveal anything. We don't need nerds with microscopes. We need nerds with gene-sequencers."

"And there are none in the Underground?"

"No, Claire. Come on. Don't tell Nikki I said this, but those idiots are mostly just hippies with nothing better to do than rattle their bongs and act like hypocrites. They drink blood just like the rest of us because (let's face it) we're *all* fucking monsters. The only issue they can even hang their hat on is the inbreeding thing lately where the humans keep getting sick. They're barely worthy of having a Fangbook page. You know that."

Claire rolled her eyes — a mannerism that hadn't changed since she'd been forty years younger, since her face had been fifteen years younger. She'd grown into a pretty young (-ish) woman, petite and lithe and with a charming non-fanged smile that she accented with falsies whenever she went out. But when she did things like roll her eyes, Reginald couldn't help but think of the little girl in the coat with the anorak hood, content to invite a vampire into her house as long as he kept her company while her mother was too drunk to care.

"Some resistance," she said.

"They shuffle paperwork. You just wait; one day they're going to rise up with a heinous bake sale fundraiser and will propose lobby reform. It'll be chaos."

Claire sighed, then moved into the kitchen. She opened a cabinet and pulled out a box of Snaco Triscuit clones. She held the box toward Reginald and shook it.

"No thanks."

"I have taquitos, too. The non-blood kind."

"Claire, you know I don't eat that stuff anymore," he said. "I haven't eaten human food since the end of the war."

"You don't *ever* eat it? Even when you're home alone and nobody is watching?"

Reginald shrugged. He simply wasn't interested in those old habits anymore. He was a vampire, and keeping that in mind after the war had seemed important — especially given how endangered traditional vampires were these days. How many modern vampires had ever hunted? How many ran anywhere when they could drive in light-tight vehicles? How many knew how to glamour? There was no point, seeing as few modern vampires had ever seen a human up close and would probably be afraid of them if they did. Vampires these days didn't even think of themselves as fast or strong because they moved at the same speed as their neighbors. With no basis for comparison, vampiric speed, strength, sight, hearing, vision, and even sex had simply become the norm. Reginald had seen vampire porn. It didn't interest him because it looked like it was on fast-forward.

"No, not ever."

"But it's *your* company. It's how you made your fat stacks of cash."

"Yeah, well," Reginald said, "sometimes I feel like a disillusioned mother who wonders at the horror of what she's given birth to."

Claire ignored the statement's implications. "You just get sick of it, being around it all day?"

"I guess." He didn't want to talk about it. It wasn't that he felt like he was better than other vampires; he just didn't want to be like them. At all.

Claire shrugged and popped one of the crackers into her mouth. "Well, for a race that doesn't need this food, you did a pretty good job of replicating it. And thank God. Because if I couldn't eat human food openly, I'd have to move out into the wildlands with my mom. And it kind of sucks out there."

"How *is* your mom?" Reginald asked.

Claire popped another cracker. "Old."

"She doing okay?"

Claire shook her head side to side, pursing her lips in a shit-happens sort of expression. "Not really."

"I'm sorry."

"She's over eighty in a post-healthcare society. She's just old, Reginald. It's okay, really." She paused, suddenly thoughtful. "You know, the strange thing is that neither of us mind the fact that she's dying because dying is at least a *change*. You haven't changed even one little bit in the time I've known you. Neither has Nikki. To tell the truth, I find the idea of getting old and dying one day strangely comforting. It's funny: I never liked change growing up. I wanted everything to always stay the same forever — other than, of course, getting a little bigger so kids would stop picking on me. But when you spend this long watching perpetual sameness, change starts to look good again. It's like reading a good book. Good books are only good if they eventually have an end."

"Deep."

Claire shrugged and ate another cracker.

"I think it's funny that you don't think anything has changed," said Reginald, suddenly aware that he was procrastinating. Claire's mind might flit from thing to thing, but Reginald remembered perfectly well why Claire had called him — and he also remembered just how nervous her voice had sounded on the phone. She seemed calm now, but his mind was still clanging with those two simple words that had chilled him to his already-chilled bones: *It's starting.*

Claire shrugged. "Meh. So what? Dark buildings. Dark cars. Sun blockers and UV domes. Blood on the shelves in the supermarket..."

"... decimation of the world's population. A takeover by monsters. *Mad Max* style living outside of the city perimeter..."

"Like I said, no big deal," Claire finished. She slid into the big chair opposite him, her posture slumped and terrible. She was chronologically in her fifties, looked like a twenty-something, and acted like a teenager. Reginald half expected her to turn end-for-end on the chair so that her feet were up and her head was down, then pick up a phone and talk to her friends about boys and going to the mall. If, that was, the world had still had human malls and non-feral human boys.

After a quiet moment, Reginald said, "Okay. So I'm here because you called me. Sounding kind of panicked, by the way."

"I did."

"Well, what are you feeling right now?"

Claire didn't bother to sit up. She remained slumped. "Alert."

"Alert?"

"Yes, Reginald. Alert. Awake."

"Hell, *I'm* awake."

"In my head, I mean. In my chest. In my arms. Hell, in my ass. My ass is totally awake now, Reginald."

"Ironic," he said. "Mine is asleep."

"I thought you felt this kind of thing too. What with the vampire codex being in your blood and all."

He shook his head. "What I have is an archive. What you have is more like a barometer. If I look in my internal files, I can tell you how Cain felt about his breakfast a zillion years ago, but if I look tomorrow, that feeling will be exactly the same. And if I *don't* look, I'm not affected by it at all."

"Was that really his name? Cain?"

"What? Oh, yeah, I think so."

"But not like... *the* Cain."

"You're changing the subject."

"You never explained it to me," she said. "You were always like, 'I don't want to talk about it, Claire.' Well, now you're asking about my ass and I think it's only right that..."

"I am not asking about your ass."

"... that you tell *me* about what *you've* got if you want *me* to do more fortune-telling for *you*. Haven't I done enough fortune-telling already? When will it be enough?"

Reginald sighed. Claire was being sarcastic, but she was telling the truth: Reginald never *had* wanted to talk about it. Once he'd had enough time to walk up and down the bloodlines — exploring the real-as-this ability to step into the memories of any vampire in history — the mythical codex had appeared in front of him, plain as day. It had always existed as a million fragments scattered throughout vampire history, but only someone with Reginald's puzzle-solving mind would ever be able to see it. But he'd already been a Chosen One once, and that experience had ended in the extermination of a planet. He'd had a second shot at it when he'd seen the first assembled pieces of the codex and had dutifully rung the alarm, but the uprising the codex warned of had never come. He refused to be fooled a third time. He didn't want the codex, and he didn't want the ability to peep into others' minds — even if that meant leaving "mental Maurice" in his brain's shadows like childhood toys stowed under the basement

17

staircase. Every person — and every vampire — deserved the privacy of his secrets. And Reginald, for his part, deserved the chance to be a nobody for a change.

"Look…" he began. Then he sighed. "Okay, fine. Yes, 'Cain' as in the first vampire, but not really 'Cain' as in the same bad boy history talks about."

"So the way the legend explains the conflict between humans and vampires…"

"It's not true. But if you try telling that to anyone in charge — if you can find anyone with enough vampire history to even *know* the legend — they'll tell you you're crazy. The children of Cain set against the children of Abel, yada yada yada. Nobody believed that old story before the war, but now it's their bible. Almost literally, because they like to think of themselves as winners. 'We beat Abel' and stuff. They could put it on a T-shirt."

"So if it isn't 'Cain vs. Abel, how is it really?"

"We're not hunter and prey. The codex says it's closer to a symbiotic relationship."

"Like leeches," said Claire.

"No…"

"Oh! Like a tapeworm."

"Gross."

"Like one of those things that hangs on sharks?"

"Claire, all of those things are parasites. Didn't you ever take a biology class?"

She nipped the corner off a faux-Triscuit. "Someone destroyed the world before I got to high school. But it's cool. There's far less reason for me to know the state capitals or the history of the Civil War nowadays. Just think of all those poor suckers who wasted their time learning about the bicameral legislature."

Reginald pointed a "gotcha" finger at her. "But see… clearly you *do* know about the bicameral legislature."

"Right. So, like, two camels."

Reginald sat back, settling into the couch. "I shared, so now it's your turn. I'll bet if you try really hard, you can do better than 'I feel awake.'"

She stared at him, annoyed.

"Look, *you* called *me*. Should I go home? Nikki had just gotten up and was starting to do nude yoga when I walked out the door, and…"

"Oh, gross." Coming from Claire's fifty-something mouth, the statement sounded bizarre. But Reginald and Nikki had always been like a second mother and father to her, so maybe her reaction was that of imagining her parents having sex — a "gross" proposition for a child of any age. Reginald's own mother had died fifteen years ago, having remained safely hidden away, and had spent her final years happily watching vampire sitcoms over a wireless connection while eating ice cream that he'd never told her was blood-flavored. But even still, after all this time, Reginald didn't want to imagine her doing nude yoga.

"I'll talk more about it if you don't tell me what you called me over to talk about," said Reginald. Then, when Claire hesitated, he said, "When she does 'downward dog,' she sticks her…"

"Fine! Okay, whatever. I don't know really how to describe it other than to say that I'm starting to know things in a way that's more conscious. I feel it like something jutting further and further out of a fog, as if it's emerging."

"Are you still scooping up new information from the internet? You used to be like a sponge when you turned on a computer."

Claire gave a sad little frown. She held a hand in the air. Her palm sparked with blue lightning, which then crawled over her skin like a living glove. Small tendrils of blue plasma reached up into the air from her fingertips, snapping out as if grabbing for something.

"A vampire named Clark just posted on Fangbook about finding an old human-era quarter on the street," she said. "The first reply comment was, 'Cool story, bro.' That post was liked by three people within the first minute. Elsewhere, a new blog was launched, just now, about vintage Star Wars figurines modified to make the creatures into vampires."

"People are still blogging?"

"Out in the wildlands, a human named Ben Kirkman was expected in WL-14 two hours ago. He's traveling from one underground settlement to another but is running late, and is worried about a woman named Candace fearing for his safety because of it."

"Where are you getting this?"

"Off the air. I don't even need a connection. Haven't for years."

"You never told me that," said Reginald.

"It's not a normal conversation topic," she said. "Besides, I made your dead cell phone talk to Maurice from Antarctica during the war. How is that any less ridiculous?"

"You just seem sad about it."

"I can't shut it out," she said. "Back then I at least needed a computer if I was to get new information. Today, it just comes to me. I'm like an antenna. I hear *everything*. Anything transmitted electronically is very easy, but I can often pick up random thoughts at closer distances. Signals on the other side of the world are harder to hear than anything in this country or especially inside the city, but I can hear them if I try. I don't even have to use satellites. I feel as if I'm bending the energy around the curvature of the planet."

"But how?"

"How can you see into the thoughts and memories of the entire vampire family tree?"

Reginald nodded. "Touché."

They sat for a minute — the vampire who'd made his fortune by treating vampires like humans and the girl who seemed to be something other than human.

"Reginald?" she finally said.

He looked over at Claire, her long, light brown hair stubbornly trying to make its way in front of her delicate features as she fought to keep it back behind her ears. She was regarding him with a graveness that looked almost innocent. She'd grown up too damn fast. She'd never had a chance to just be a girl — to play with other girls and run around giggling about boys she liked. It wasn't fair. But at least she was here and alive, which was more than could be said for the girls she might have done that giggling with.

"What is it like for you? When you do… whatever it is? Is it as swimmy and indistinct for you as I describe it is for me?"

He considered demurring, but then found himself sighing and simply answering the question.

"I can go into their memories. And when I do, it almost feels like I'm in their bodies."

"Can you go into Nikki?"

Reginald resisted making a joke.

"I try to stay out of anyone who's alive now. Walking the blood memories of ancient ancestors feels different from peeping into the thoughts of living vampires. I can usually only do that close up, only if I feel I have to, and only if they don't try to keep me out. It seems to be easier with vampires I'm closely related to."

"Like your maker."

Reginald held her gaze. "Yes."

"So you can feel Maurice."

"His memories. A mental impression of him."

"Do you still miss him?"

Reginald looked down. Which of the thousand answers he'd felt over the years should he give her? Yes, he missed Maurice. Yes, he felt guilty about Maurice's death, seeing as it had been Reginald's mission that had brought it about. And yes, even though it wasn't fair, he sometimes blamed Claire for sending him on that mission. Forty years hadn't dulled the pain one bit. Nikki had grieved for a while, and Brian, who was Maurice's only other progeny, had grieved for much longer. But even Brian had eventually gone on, because Brian didn't have to sense Maurice's thoughts every time he laid still at night like Reginald did. Maurice was always near Reginald. *Always.* He was a hair's breadth away — close enough to hear as if in an echo, but never close enough. Having Maurice's blood memories in his head was almost torture for Reginald. It was like having a conversation with a recording: he could talk to his maker forever, but Maurice could never really, truly, autonomously talk back, because he was gone. And on top of everything, Reginald felt the terrible guilt of neglect. He could sense Maurice's thoughts inside him, and hearing those thoughts was terrible. So for most of the past forty years he'd refused to listen, shutting Maurice away and pretending he couldn't hear him scratching at the walls of his mental box.

"Yes, I still miss him."

"I do too."

After a long moment, Reginald decided to try again. Sometimes cracking Claire's prescient code was like water eroding stone. You just had to keep plinking away.

"On the phone," he began, "you said that 'it was starting.'"

She nodded, now looking down. The mood in the room had soured. He didn't know how it had happened — maybe the talk of Maurice had done it — but it had. It was a good thing. It meant that Claire's time-honed defenses were finally ratcheting back, that the two of them were finally approaching the thing that Claire had been panicked enough to call about before she'd convinced herself that everything was just fine.

"Is it the humans?" he asked.

Pause. "Yes."

"What about them?"

She shook her head, now looking at her hands. Her light manner was gone, and Reginald felt himself shiver. He was already warring with his own defenses and demons, realizing what she might have meant when she'd called — and how that might change everything.

"What *about* the humans?" he repeated.

"You know."

"Some sort of an..." He swallowed. It wasn't true. It couldn't be true. He'd finally made peace with the fact that it had *never* been true. But he had to finish the sentence, and he did it like ripping off a Band-Aid: "... an uprising?"

Claire shrugged, still not looking up. "Maybe and maybe not. More than anything, I get the sense of a sleeping machine finally starting up. It has the feeling of... of *dawning.*"

"Where are you getting this? What's telling you that something is coming?"

She waved her finger in the air, presumably indicating all of the signals she was picking up on her internal antenna, then assembling like her own kind of codex. "Everything," she said.

"How? Where?"

"I don't know."

"Could I glamour you? Get it out that way?"

She laughed without humor. "Reginald, do you realize that I could glamour *you* now?"

His shoulders slumped. "If all you know is 'something is coming' but nothing specific and present, then why did you call me?"

"Because you needed to know," she said.

"But *what* do I need to know? Give me something I can use, Claire!"

"I don't have anything more. Not yet. I just know that something is coming together. When it comes, it comes."

Reginald shook his head. He should be used to this from her, but he wasn't. "You're not helping, Claire," he said.

She smiled. "Just stay here for a while, okay?" she said. "Watch some TV with me."

"Remember how we used to watch *Columbo*?"

"*Columbo* is what I had in mind, actually," she said.

He laughed. "Human TV? Good luck finding it on the vampire network."

With that, Claire's television turned on, and a feature began playing despite the fact that the TV didn't even appear to be plugged in.

Claire tapped her head. "Turns out, Merlin remembers every episode."

SINCE THE FALL OF HUMANITY, day and night had taken on a strange reversal. The world was alive at night and asleep during the day. Lawns were mowed and watered at night. Barbecues and parties were held at night. Some vampires worked the day shift and drove home in light-tight cars, but they did so with their stereos off or low, their wheeled transgressions kept respectful. Daytime was for sleeping. Daytime hours were quiet hours. A few cars passed while Reginald thought about Claire's prediction, knowing it might come in minutes, hours, days, or never.

Claire had fallen asleep while faultlessly reconstructing episodes of *Columbo* for them to watch. She'd been using her archival memory to broadcast images to the TV like a wireless video recorder, and as she'd begun to drift, the action onscreen had become stranger — and, Reginald suspected, not entirely true to the original versions. He didn't remember Columbo fighting a dragon. He didn't remember Columbo pondering an asteroid approaching the Earth and then watching a giant space serpent devour it. Just before Claire had fallen asleep, Columbo had looked up at the sky and said in his gravelly voice, "Well, this ain't good." The screen had gone to snow soon after, and Reginald had gotten up to lay a blanket across the sleeping young woman who wasn't really a young woman. Then he'd turned off the TV, because leaving it on might give him access to her dreams. He didn't want that. Claire was one of only a few people whose thoughts he couldn't read, and the sense of mental quiet he always had around her was refreshing.

He crossed Claire's living room and touched a button on the wall to display an exterior image on a small monitor. The yard was bright with long shadows, the sun barely past its rise. The streets were mostly empty, though a few blackout cars were making their way through the quiet intersection at the corner. He'd gotten used to the sense of reversal over the years. The preternatural quiet that used to exist only at night had simply shifted twelve hours. If you were awake in the middle of the afternoon these days, it meant you had insomnia. And if you were awake because you worked the day shift, you'd get paid double for the hazard and inconvenience of doing so.

Claire, living incognito amongst vampires, had adopted their sleep schedule. Reginald looked over at her covered form on the couch and suddenly felt sorry for her. She had all the knowledge in the world — almost literally — but could do nothing of value with it. Reginald had once asked Claire what life was like inside her head. She'd said it was *loud*. She got along as well as she could, but Nikki and Reginald and Brian were the only people she truly trusted. Even the wild humans hiding out in the wildlands didn't understand Claire because she didn't light up their body heat sensors. Reginald kept trying to get her to move out to the secret stronghold where her mother lived, but she kept declining, saying she'd never fit in. She felt she had a job to do in the city, she said. She had to be here, in the heart of the beast. She had to be ready, because unlike Reginald, she'd never given up on the future. She had to stand guard, watching and waiting like a tired keeper outside a sacred crypt. And now, it seemed as if whatever Claire had been waiting for might be coming true after all.

Reginald watched Claire sleep, wondering how many lives he'd screwed up by becoming a vampire. He'd screwed up his own for sure, plus Nikki's. He'd made things harder for Maurice, both by being turned as a sub-standard recruit and later by getting him killed. He'd thrown a wrench in Claire's life by stalking and then befriending her — although according to Claire, his own actions mattered little because they'd been destined to meet. And of course there was the small matter of the entire human population, who were now either dead or imprisoned as blood slaves. What kind of a Chosen One was he?

Suddenly, without warning, Claire sat up. In one moment she went from dozing to fully awake, now staring at Reginald with wide eyes. Everything in her seemed to be churning. Reginald could hear the very blood surging through her veins. Her *human* blood. Her *incubus* blood. Her *hybrid* blood, which seemed to know what it was, what it wasn't, and what it was here to do.

"It's begun," she said to Reginald, her lower lip shaking. "It's finally begun, and now you have to stop it."

THREE

Grey Dawn

Of course, he *couldn't* stop it. He didn't even know what "it" was until the rest of the world did.

As soon as Claire yelled at him to go, Reginald extended the sunport on Claire's front door until it made a seal against the door of his car in the driveway, then ran through the long tube and climbed in. He activated the car's screens, backed out, hit Claire's mailbox, scuffed his tire on the curb, and peeled away.

The streets were empty. He stopped, suddenly aware that Claire hadn't told him where to go. They'd gotten so used to communicating in hints and doubletalk and mental metaphors that she'd simply given him the command and he'd followed it without question. It wasn't until he was three miles down the road that he realized he had no idea where he was going. So with no better ideas in mind, he drove recklessly across town, panicked about something completely unknown, and pulled into his own garage. The garage door took forever to seal against the concrete, and then his doors finally disengaged and he tumbled out in a pile. He picked himself off the floor, rushed in, and found

Nikki just where he'd left her, doing the same thing she'd been doing when he'd left.

"I've been gone for eight hours," he said, temporarily forgetting his rush at the sight of his naked wife doing yoga.

Nikki was on her back. She arched into a bridge, her breasts pointing perkily upward. "This is a long routine," she said.

"I was at Claire's."

"I know. You told me when you left."

"She says hi," he told her. He said it as if annoyed that she was forcing him to engage in pleasantries, when in fact she'd done nothing of the kind. Claire also hadn't requested that Reginald tell Nikki "Hi." He'd totally made it up.

"Well," said Nikki, bending her arms and settling into a neck bridge, "hi back."

Reginald watched her, his earlier urgency dissipating as he realized he'd just crossed a lot of unalarmed streets in order to find an unalarmed woman doing yoga. Nikki did a lot of yoga. A lot, lot, lot of yoga. She seemed to do it in order to infuriate herself. She was a vampire who'd been made from a woman in excellent shape, and no matter how much practice she undertook, she'd never permanently elongate or strengthen any muscles. The exercises were pointless. Nikki said she did them because they hurt and because, if you were masochistic, you could do them forever. The problem with eternity, in Nikki's opinion, was running out of things to do — and that was especially true when the cities were partitioned off, when you couldn't hunt without a permit, when you couldn't stretch your legs in the wild open spaces if you hoped someday to be allowed back inside. Wild humans (the few thousand the patrols never managed to wipe out in the purge) could be dangerous, and nobody wanted to take the risk of allowing pests to enter the city.

Nikki was still looking at him. But her angle was wrong and she couldn't see him properly, so she kicked her legs off the ground. She rolled sideways until she was up on one hand, her body erect.

"Why are you so sweaty?" she asked.

"Claire," he said. He was starting to remember his earlier urgency, figuring he should at least check the TV before stopping to gawk at nudity.

"I'm Nikki," Nikki clarified.

"Claire says it's starting."

"What's starting?"

"The human thing."

Nikki rolled down, settling back into her bridge. "Oh."

Reginald felt something inside himself droop. Nikki tried to be kind about Reginald's occasional prophetic quirks, but after forty years, the false alarms had worn her thin and she no longer believed. It even made sense; he himself didn't believe most of the time. But every once in a while he'd decide to tinker with the codex like an old man tinkering with an old hobby, and diving fresh into the blood always left him sure he'd missed something and that doom was still coming. But it never did, never had — and, they both felt sure in Reginald's rational moments, never would.

"It's true this time," Reginald said, realizing how lame he must look and sound. "Claire told me."

Nikki came down onto her back, then stood and donned a robe. She walked up to Reginald but didn't take his hands as he'd thought she would.

"We've been through this," she said.

Her calm voice made Reginald suddenly furious. She

was talking to him the way you'd talk to a mental patient who was beyond the capacity to understand.

"Dammit, Nikki," he spat. He stepped away from her and began searching the couch, the coffee table, the kitchen countertop. Then he looked at her and said, "Where is the remote?"

Nikki had it in the pocket of her robe. She handed it to him without comment. He clicked on the TV, then flipped past a talk show and an obscene vampire sitcom. He stopped on VNN, which showed an overhead view of a factory in the daytime. It was labeled as a live shot and the audio track was nothing but the whipping sound of helicopter rotors. The rotor noise was loud, probably because there would need to be two of them to support the weight of the helicopter's metal sun shielding.

"There," he said, pointing at the TV.

"It's a factory."

He pointed to a caption toward the bottom of the screen. "It's a blood farm. See? I told you."

"I'm sure it's just another piece worrying why the human stock keeps getting sick," she said.

"You'll see."

Nikki gave him a look. The look wasn't angry. It was, if anything, pityingly compassionate. It was the look you'd give a slow person who wanted to record a rock song because he thought it would top the charts.

"Don't look at me that way," he said. "Which one of us possesses the vampire codex?"

"I seem to remember spending months looking for that codex myself," she said. "And yet, it wasn't there when we opened the crypt."

"It's here! It's in me!"

"Reginald..."

He turned to the TV, then increased the volume. The

video switched back and forth between shots of the blood farm from overhead, shots of the blood farm from a distance on the ground, and shots of two newspeople in a busy newsroom wearing sufficient makeup so as to appear less dead on camera. In the overhead shot, a fire was now visible billowing from one side of the huge, warehouse-style building. In the ground shot, smoke from the same fire rose in a vertical black column. The camera zoomed in, into shadows visible through one end of the hanger-like doors. There were humans around the doors, in the sun, holding them open. Deeper in the shadows, the blurs of vampires could be seen leaping from end to end. As Reginald watched, something small popped like a balloon and spilled red paint. But of course, it wasn't paint.

Nikki's demeanor changed. She sat on the edge of the couch and listened. Reginald listened beside her, turning the TV up further, now catching the story as the anchors began speaking.

The facility, it turned out, was the MorningFresh blood farm, located just outside the US vampire core in New York City. Apparently there'd been some sort of a rebellion, with the human captives rising up to seize power from the vampire guards.

Nikki gasped.

Rebellions had been common when the first blood farms had been established after the war, when wild human populations had still existed in vampire-controlled territory. Back then, humans had still outnumbered their vampires neighbors more than twenty-to-one, and due to the peculiar breed of blindness that affects humans in dire situations, they had still been holding out hope that they could turn things around and win the human-vampire war. So when the first farms were established by the governorships in order to ensure that the growing vampire population and the dwindling human population didn't end up in a food shortage, humans had fought the new businesses tooth and nail — both from inside the farms and from outside, as rescue crews attempted to penetrate the external security. Many human stock had to be killed. For some strange reason during those conflicts (a reason Reginald had blamed on yet more arbitrary supernatural rules established by angels and their ilk, like "humans can't be glamoured into slavery"), glamouring didn't often take on human blood stock and never held permanently.

But that had been a long time ago. Today's blood farms were nothing like those first tentative ones. Forty years ago, humans had to be strapped down tight before they could be drained through IV lines, and hippie human rights groups like Nikki's had had a heyday. But in time, as new generations of humans were born into captivity, blood stock began to accept their situations as normal and they stopped fighting. Blood farming was opened to private enterprise, and companies like MorningFresh moved into the previously-government-only space and made a big deal about treating humans humanely. They allowed their populations to live in contained, closely watched communities that almost resembled the primitive communities from the human past. Rebellions (or even mildly insurgent behavior) had all but vanished, and when problems arose, a round of glamouring was usually a sufficient answer. When Reginald had learned this last bit, it had chilled him. If humans couldn't normally be glamoured into slavery, then the fact that glamouring *could* subdue farm humans today implied something terrible: that they no longer even thought of themselves as slaves.

Nikki watched, her hand on her open mouth. Once upon a time, bloodshed hadn't been shocking to either of them — to *any* of them, all across the world. But all of the bloodshed these days went into tubes and pouches, and thinking about what must be going on inside the farm's main building made even Reginald's prophetic hair stand on end.

The cameras continued to flip from view to view as the situation slowly unfolded.

As Nikki and Reginald watched, they saw blurs and blood and fire and smoke. There were several brief interviews with local vampires who told reporters how shocked they were, saying that they used to talk to some of the more intelligent humans through the fences — and, when the guards would allow it, to toss them food. The Morning-Fresh facility was spacious and clean. The stock there had always seemed so docile. Yet earlier in the day, a troop of humans were being led from their pens to the milking chamber by MorningFresh techs (not even *handlers*; Morning-Fresh was a civilized workplace where animosity wasn't usually necessary) when several of the stock had pulled homemade wooden shivs from their clothing and had staked the techs. The guards had taken a few startled moments to react, and those few seconds had been enough for another group of humans to come up behind the guards and string garrotes made of old silver jewelry around their necks. Using the silver, they'd wrangled the guards to the ground, ripped off their armor, and staked them, too.

That was all the reporter on the scene seemed to know. The initial report had come from a tech who'd escaped, and what had happened since then was anybody's guess. From what the camera could see, the vampire guards seemed to have rallied, but Reginald had committed the layouts of MorningFresh (and every other new building he'd been able to find blueprints for) to memory, and he felt less sure that they'd regained control. In the camera's shot, he could see that only the outer doors of the factory were open. The inner doors, thirty yards further in, were still closed. What they were seeing were only a few combatants dueling it out in an oversized foyer. Anything could be happening in the factory itself.

"What do you think happened?" said Nikki when the loop repeated again and the reporter began telling them what they already knew.

"I'd say the humans got tired of being stuck with needles and kept in cages," said Reginald.

But before they could think on it for long, more breaking news began to intrude on the MorningFresh story. There had, it seemed, been an attack on a vampire city a hundred miles from the blood farm using a kind of Trojan horse explosive. The explosive, according to reports, had been embedded with silver shrapnel and encased in several nested wooden crates. It had been pushed into an indoor market, disguised as a freight shuttle, and detonated. Several vampires had been impaled and killed instantly, and medics were still attempting to cut silver out of a dozen others.

But there was more: in Arizona, a second rebellion had occurred at a factory that did pre-processing for HemoByte blood supplements. The factory used human labor (it was a notch above slavery; captive humans could do menial jobs in exchange for credits they could later redeem for small luxuries), and as had happened at MorningFresh, several workers had seized vampire supervisors using old silver jewelry. Early reports indicated that the supervisors had then been shoved into a massive centrifuge the facility used to separate the red blood cells used in HemoByte pills from plasma and platelets.

And lastly — for now, anyway — the wall of a vampire city that had been fortified in the bones of Detroit was on fire, now being held by humans carrying crossbows. The guards in the city were managing to fight back somewhat, but they had to do so while wearing lead daysuits, and each city only had so many.

"Claire was right," said Reginald. "It's starting."

Nikki seemed irritated by Reginald's vindicated tone. "What exactly, Reginald? *What's* starting?"

"The second phase of the war."

Nikki shook her head. "It's just insurgence. They'll knock it back." Which, come to think of it, was a strange thing for her to say. Nikki was part of a vampire resistance that, in theory, should welcome anything that disrupted the status quo. But the way she was reacting just spoke to the group's irrelevance. It spoke to a group that only protested in order to hear itself protest.

Reginald pointed at the TV. He didn't see how she could dismiss any of what she was seeing with a straight face.

"*Four* incidents, Nikki. In *four* cities. *At the same time.*"

As if on cue, the reporter onscreen touched her ear. Then she held the mic to her lips, looked into the camera, and said, "I'm being told that a bus filled with photobombs has been left in front of the EUVC parliament building in Geneva, and a human group is threatening to detonate it," she said. "Going to our Geneva affiliate now."

The Geneva reporter — a man with jet black hair wearing a jet black suit — was standing in a kind of long dark tube. The shot gave the impression of staring down a hallway, and at the end of the hallway, in the sun, was a large city bus standing in the middle of a deserted square. The reporter was sweating as scant ultraviolet made its way down toward him.

Nikki gasped.

Reginald forgot his irritation as he watched Nikki react.

She wasn't gasping at the bus or the implication of the photobombs — human Anti-Vampire Taskforce blow-and-illuminate weapons that hadn't been seen for decades. She was gasping at the daylight that was painting the square in the distance.

"They have a sun blocker," she said.

"Apparently not anymore," said Reginald.

His keen eyes, peering at the large high-definition TV, picked out dozens of piles of ash visible all around the sun-lit square. Geneva, like the USVC's home city of New York, was usually protected by the massive, geosynchronously orbiting shield that had been assembled in space twenty years ago. Both cities — the vampire world's two major hubs — operated 24 hours a day in permanent night.

Or at least, they used to.

Reginald's mind barely registered the deaths that must have occurred already this morning — or already this afternoon across the ocean. It was focused instead on logistics, consulting the collected vampire knowledge that was resident in his brain. Battle gears that had been long dormant began to turn.

There had been at least five incidents, and more might be in progress or forthcoming. If you counted whatever had been done to the sun blocker (Reginald's guess was computer-based sabotage; it seemed unlikely that the humans had actually gotten into space), then there were six. The fog of war would mean that until this wave passed — *if* it passed — they wouldn't be able to accurately tally the damage because there'd be too much panic and misinformation. The best they could do would be a guess — and right now, a guess wasn't good enough.

Reginald needed data. Not gossip, not hearsay, and not second-hand accounts. *Data*.

Nikki gripped his arm, the pressure of all five digits suddenly betraying her need for his support. It was strange. There had been frightening times in their shared past, but even when she'd been afraid, she'd always held her own. He hadn't seen her truly vulnerable since she'd been human. Nikki had lost her parents early and as a result had put up a solid wall for the rest of her human life. Weakness, she'd learned, could be deadly. But now here that weakness was, and Reginald couldn't fault her one iota for it.

"It's a *bus*," Nikki said, looking at the TV. "Why did nobody think a *bus* was suspicious?"

"They use buses in Geneva," Reginald told her. "New York too."

"You're kidding."

"And subways. Why are you surprised? We have a car."

"Well..." she began, but didn't finish. Reginald felt a frown forming on his lips. It was impossible not to sense some of the old feelings returning. He'd been a vampire for longer than he'd been a human, but 42 years (80 if you counted from his birth) compared to a vampire's potential lifespan was nothing, and he was barely faster or stronger today than he'd been when he was first turned. On his first vampire night with Maurice, Reginald had managed a pushup and a slow jog. Today he could place highly in a human marathon and lift around three hundred pounds, but both feats could be outdone by a fit human. Reginald having a car was like a handicapped person having a wheelchair. It didn't make him feel any more like he belonged.

"City-dwellers are apparently as lazy as I am," he said, a bit more harshly than he'd intended.

"I didn't mean it that way," she said, loosening the

pressure on his arm and turning it into an affectionate hold. Then she looked at him appraisingly, continuing when she deemed it safe. "But it does seem strange. Vampires taking buses."

"A lot of things are strange these days, Nik," he said with a sigh.

He looked at the screen, watching the station flip between the five incidents. The shot of the bus bomb caught his attention, and he wondered if vampire troops had reappropriated the robots that were once used by human bomb squads. There would be little point to robots under normal circumstances; unless bombs flung wood or silver or unless the shrapnel threatened to result in beheading, explosions were little more than annoyances. Even the carnage on VNN was strangely clean. Other than the screaming vampires who'd taken shards of silver, none of the news footage was remotely gut-churning. Vampires were hard to *wound*. They either died and became bland piles of ash, or they healed instantly.

As if to prove the point, the shot flipped to show a reporter speaking to one of the wood-bomb victims. The caption at the bottom of the screen read: "Sally Thornton — lost left arm in Seattle blast." But Sally was currently summoning someone off-camera using impatient gestures of both arms, and where her left side had been blown away, her shirt was torn open and a boob hung out.

"We evolved right onto the chopping block," said Reginald, a realization dawning.

Nikki looked over.

"Everyone wondered why the angels never showed up to give us a high-five for winning the war," he continued. "Why was that? Because hey, we'd done what they wanted, right? We tipped the scales on the humans. Then we evolved, as instructed. Look, Nik." He pointed at the TV screen. "We even took back the day. We've got our tunnels, or blackout vehicles, our lead defense suits, our orbiting space shades. We've got HemoByte and humanely farmed blood. We're so damn evolved we don't have to hunt or kill anymore. And now look at us: right out in the sun when the curtain is pulled back."

They both looked at the screen. The station was showing Geneva again, and the piles of ash visible in the square put an exclamation point on Reginald's sentence. The vampires in the city had gotten so used to going out whenever they wanted that they must have been taken totally off guard when the sun suddenly came out.

"Wait until night," said Nikki. "The CPC will find whoever's responsible."

"I don't know about that," said Reginald. "They've grown too dull."

Nikki looked at him like he'd shredded her favorite teddy bear. He could sense the tone of her thoughts despite trying not to, and knew that she was starting to believe what he'd said earlier. She was starting to see how coordinated the human actions were, and how this was bigger than five isolated acts of terrorism. Humans were supposed to be watched and contained. Groups in the wilds were supposed to be followed by satellites, tracked, and exterminated when they got too big. The humans were supposed to only have the communities the vampires allowed them to have, and now it looked like they'd found a way to have one much larger. Reginald couldn't help but worry about the power of human coordination. The vampires had created little themselves; they'd built almost all of what they had on what suddenly felt like shaky, co-opted ground. What might humans know about the vampires' world that even vampires didn't know? It was human technology that had launched the New York and Geneva sun blockers, human technology that broadcast vampire television, and human networks that made Fangbook accessible anywhere. The humans had made it all, and now he feared they might be trying to take it back.

"What do you mean?" said Nikki.

"We *needed* the humans," said Reginald. "They sharpened us. When they were in charge and we were in the shadows, we had to fight and hunt. Today we don't have to do any of that, and we've gotten soft. Now *they're* the species in the shadows. Now *we've* sharpened *them*." He turned to look into Nikki's eyes. "And now I'm afraid that our lazy, decadent necks are going to get cut."

"You're making too much of it," she said. But meeting her eyes, he could tell that she was only saying the words in order to try to convince herself.

"I don't think so," he said.

"Is this opinion coming from the vampire codex?"

"It's coming from common sense."

"And from Claire?"

"From inevitability."

Nikki tried to sit up tall. "We're still vampires," she said.

"Yes, we are," said Reginald. His head turned toward the TV. "But what have *they* become?"

FOUR

Assholes

Reginald got a phone call. He wasn't surprised.

"No," he told the phone. "No fucking way."

The phone rallied back, trying to be passive-aggressive: "You *have* to. You *have* to help."

"No, I don't," Reginald said. "You've raised your petard. Prepare to be hoisted upon it."

The voice said nothing, clearly failing to understand. So Reginald added, "Would you prefer a metaphor wherein you get fucked up the ass by a dildo that you your-self created?"

On the other end of the line, Charles Barkley cleared his throat. This had to be difficult for Charles. Reginald had been an outsider with the vampire government from the start, and he'd been an outsider with Charles from the moment they'd laid eyes on each other, back in the bowling alley where Reginald had first been turned. Charles had probably drawn the short straw to have to make this call — or maybe Timken had made him do it, reasoning that Reginald and Charles shared a connection. Bygones, after all these years, would surely be bygones. Sure, Charles had tried to kill Reginald a few times, but at the end of the human world, weren't they all ultimately on the same team?

"Look," said Barkley in a pouty voice. "Just do it."

"Oh, well, after a persuasive argument like that, how can I refuse?"

"We'll pay you for your time."

"I don't need your money," said Reginald. "I'm incredibly rich. Turns out, fat sells."

"Come on. This is the future of our race we're talking about."

"Is it?" said Reginald, switching the phone to his other ear. "Well, then whoopity fucking doo; I'd better snap-to and help out! Vampirism has been *so great* to me. I was turned into a vampire against my will, then tried and persecuted, then almost executed. I saved the world and everyone hated me for it, and when I tried to make peace after being chased out and almost killed, everyone laughed at me. I tried to stop your fucking regime and ended up causing the apocalypse instead, and…"

"I don't think you can take credit for that," Barkley interjected.

"… and when it was all over, your buddy's right-hand man killed my best friend and maker. And then what happened? Well, as a final insulting capper, I finally embraced my nature as the world's big fat joke and found out that junk food sells… but when I saw all of you fuckers starting to eat it, I lost my taste for it. Now I only drink blood, and I run. Everyone else eats junk and does nothing all day, and somehow *I'm* still the outcast. And surprise, surprise… 180 degrees later and here we are again with *you* fucked and *me* expected to save the day. So what can you possibly offer to tempt me, Charles? What will make it worth my while to humiliate myself further? Because I've

43

been telling you all for *years* that a human uprising was coming and that you'd better prepare — 'watch them closely,' I said; 'don't get complacent and assume they'll lie down forever,' I said — but nobody's ever listened… and now, when you finally *do* want to listen, do you really expect me to believe that the 'solution' you want from me won't involve killing and torturing a bunch more people?"

"To be clear, we don't believe your bullshit about the human revolution," said Charles.

"Really."

"Not at all. We want advice on how to quell an insurgence."

"Do it your motherfucking self, Charles."

Charles clucked his tongue on the other end of the line. "You sure have grown up," he said. "Such a mouth you've developed. You weren't like this when you were Maurice's pet."

Reginald felt his face redden. Charles had managed to insult both him and Maurice in one backhanded comment, and he'd done it while asking Reginald's strategic mind for help. But rising to his bait wouldn't be the right choice. In over forty years of dealing with Charles — and almost another forty years before that of dealing with people just *like* Charles — he'd learned that you couldn't actually fight fire with fire. Snapping back at Charles would only make things worse.

"Have a nice life, Councilman Barkley."

Charles huffed, but then Reginald heard activity on the other end of the phone. A voice in the background told Charles to let him try, and Reginald prepared himself to listen to more bullshit from some other loudmouth government asswipe.

"Re-gggggie," said the voice that came onto the phone, drawing his loathed nickname out into two long syllables.

"Who is this?" Reginald asked. But it was just a stalling tactic. He knew exactly who he was talking to. He remembered vocal patterns as perfectly as he remembered everything else.

"I'm hurt," said the voice. As he said it, Reginald could imagine a cleft chin and tombstone-white teeth curling into a dramatic frown.

"I die, and then the world ends," said Reginald, "and still somehow I have to deal with you."

"Hey. We shared a coffee machine and glances at chicks in working-girl stockings. Am I right?"

"I'm hanging up, Todd."

"Hey," said Walker's smooth voice. "Remember Noel?" She could've been hot if she'd ever done herself up right."

"I remember Noel," said Reginald. "I found her hand under the copier and set it next to the rest of her body after you killed her, so that she could be buried intact."

"I didn't kill Noel," said Walker.

"Scott, then."

"Okay, I killed Scott. But I was a kid with a machine gun that first night. Wasn't it like that when you were newly turned?"

"What do you want, Todd?"

"I want you to come to New York, same as Chuckie does. We'll take in a show." This was a joke. Most of New York was deserted even at night because the vampire population was so small and hence was safer in a cluster. The city had proven impossible to clear, even forty years later, because it was simply too large and the human bands in the old neighborhoods kept moving around. So the US Vampire Council had walled off the southern tip of Manhattan and fortified the USVC building in the financial district, and it had let the rest of the city go feral. Broadway had gone with it. The only "shows" still playing in the vampire section of New York were sex shows, of which Walker probably partook often.

"Fuck you."

"Come on. We'll make it worth your while."

"I have all the money I'll ever need," Reginald said. It was true, too. After the vampire government had gotten the presses going and re-minted world currency to replace the scattered currencies of the human world, the system had stabilized surprisingly fast, and Mogul Reginald had cornered more than his share.

"Hey," said Walker, chuckling. "How is Nikki?"

Reginald was taken off guard. He didn't reply.

"You're married, right? How is she?"

"Fine."

"Just to be clear, I meant 'How IS she.' *IS*. You know what I'm saying." He chuckled with sexual innuendo.

Reginald prepared to hang up.

"She was so hot. I'll bet she's really wild, too. And totally fucking tight. You know what I mean by…"

"Tell Charles I said I fucked his mother," said Reginald, taking the phone away from his cheek.

"And with her being in the Underground?" Walker continued, his voice now sounding canned with the phone no longer against Reginald's ear. He made panting noises. "Seriously, revolutionary chicks are so hot. I can just imagine Nikki firing a gun. Just a regular human *gun*. You know, so the recoil makes her tits bounce."

Reginald stopped with his finger hovering above the END button. He put the phone back to his ear.

"What was that?"

"Oh, come on. I heard you never miss anything. I'll bet you heard me unbuckle my pants a minute ago so I could beat off thinking about your wife."

Reginald felt his fangs extend. He was suddenly sure he could lift a house. "I'll kill you," he said.

"Good. I'm in New York. Come here and maybe we won't send CPC to arrest Nikki as a subversive."

"They don't even do anything," said Reginald. "They're just lobbyists and paper-pushers."

"All I know is that they're on the restricted roster," said Walker. "'Report your neighbors.' 'Anarchists are a threat to us all.' You know the slogans."

"Sounds like Claude Toussant's work," said Reginald. He hadn't heard anything about the "Report your neighbors" initiative for over thirty years, but Claude had a million zingers at the ready. One recent poster and TV propaganda campaign showed a young human boy with a sinister scowl on his face, holding a stake. The caption read: *He'll grow up to kill your family. Will you let him?*

"And that's another reason to come," said Walker, twisting the knife. "To catch up with family. Claude will be so happy to see you."

There were a million things Reginald could say to that, but he held himself back. Just as with Charles, Walker would only be egged on by anything else he said. The die was cast. If they knew about Nikki's involvement in the Underground, then he had to go. He wouldn't make it worse by opening his chest to stabbings.

"When and where?" said Reginald.

And Walker, grinning all the way through the phone line, told him.

FIVE

New York, New York

Nikki went with him. Brian went with him too. The three of them were like a posse.

Reginald didn't strictly need Nikki or Brian, but he didn't like the idea of going to see Walker without moral support. Besides, he had plenty of money to blow on the trip. So they took a shielded jet — private, because with only ten million people in the world and with half of them being slaves to the other half, there was little demand for regular commercial air traffic between any two cities. There was a daily flight from New York to Los Angeles and another from New York to Geneva (with a stopover in Paris), but the other settlements (Chicago, Berlin, the Far East Council's home city of Beijing — an abandoned city if ever there was one) were serviced once a week or less.

They landed at the bones of JFK airport near three A.M, then got into a blackout limo for the drive into the city. They traveled only on patrolled roads, but Reginald couldn't help but wonder about the wildlands beyond. New York had been home to almost as many people in its day than existed in the entire world now, and a lot of those people had run to the suburbs during the purge. CPC and other agencies claimed that they tracked humans on their satellites, but the world — even just the area outside of (and, honestly, *inside* of) New York's boroughs — was a big place. There were only a handful of vampire cities, and that left a lot of open space for human men and women to roam.

And grow.

And plan.

And reproduce.

And innovate.

As they drove, Reginald stared at the screen where the window would have been decades ago, watching as the camera showed him the city's skyline approaching in green-tinted black. He would ordinarily retract the shields for nighttime driving, but Timken had sent the limo — and, being a government vehicle, it was armored and didn't open up. So Reginald took in the view in the enclosed space as best he could, watching both the city and the deserted sprawls behind them. He wondered again what might be brewing where vampire eyes weren't watching. Reginald had spent some time tooling through the wildlands out of curiosity, and he'd seen a lot of video footage and documentaries of what the wildlands had become. All but the largest cities were now overgrown with plant life, looking like something out of a post-apocalyptic storybook — which, when you got right down to it, was exactly what they were.

The documentaries said there were isolated bands of wild humans who lived in those thickets, but Reginald had always questioned the numbers they quoted. Back before he'd begun to disbelieve the codex, he spent inordinate amounts of time trying to work out the mechanics of a human uprising. He filled notebooks with handwritten calculations out of habit, despite the fact that he could do the figuring in his head. He began to believe that there were many more humans hiding than the Vampire Nation believed — that there had to be in order for the predictions to make sense. But as he worked and panicked and tried to raise his futile, laughable alarm, the days stretched into weeks. Weeks stretched into years. Years stretched into decades. And as more time passed, it all began to seem like bullshit: the codex, the uprising, even his own math on the matter.

But now, as he looked through the windows of the limo, he realized that he *had* been wrong about those numbers — but only because his timing had been off. He'd thought the uprising prediction had been bogus because decades had passed, but now he saw that it *had* to take this long. Time needed to pass, so that humanity would be able to mature enough to strike.

Forty years.

Two human generations.

That was enough time for them to forget what they needed to forget, and turn what they needed to remember into legend. Enough time for them to learn what they needed to learn, for hatred to brew and percolate in their very blood, for them to multiply and adapt. Food in the wilds was plentiful. The soil was good, and there was a lot of wildlife. The humans had been dislocated, but they had evolved brains capable of adjusting. Their old technology, in all those abandoned cities and homes, was just lying around, waiting to be picked up. They'd have had no problem finding food and clean water. And what would they do, with those abundant supplies and nothing but time and hate on their hands? They'd grow. They'd swell. They'd train. They'd innovate. Humanity could be lazy and repugnant, but it had sharpened for forty long years under the honing edge of the vampire grindstone.

The official estimates pegged the human population at five million — half in captivity and half in the wildlands, living as slow-witted savages. But Reginald's numbers, now that he adjusted them in the limo, pointed to many more than that. He could see the unfolding of the new human societies in his mind as surely as he could predict the falling of dominoes. They'd form clusters. They'd establish hierarchy and nominate leaders. They'd have children and they'd form religions. They'd tell the old stories, and they'd find hate and fury. They'd find a reason to believe. And belief, Reginald knew, could be a powerful and dangerous thing.

The car crossed into the city, then wound through a well-lit guarded corridor carved through New York's destruction and chaos. Beyond the fences and walls, Reginald, Nikki, and Brian could see burnt-out abandoned buildings, the rusted wrecks of cars, and the detritus of old lives. Here and there, Reginald saw a human skeleton, long ago picked over. Once or twice he saw a wild human in the shadows: a quick flash of eyes in the headlights, like those of an alley cat.

The corridor took them into lower Manhattan, into the area where the old Trade Center used to be. The driver approached the USVC building and pulled into an underground garage. Then they got out of the limo and as they walked, the driver (who'd transitioned into the role of an armed escort) explained that the USVC building had been partially converted into apartments, and that they'd be staying in two of them as special guests. There were stores and restaurants and entertainment in the surrounding area (and behind the sector walls) if they wanted to explore, and the entire area was accessible 24 hours a day thanks to the orbiting sun blocker.

Nikki chuckled humorlessly when he mentioned the sun blocker, but the driver didn't seem to understand. Nikki didn't explain. She simply said that they'd accept the guest apartments in the building and that regardless of the darkness outside, they wouldn't venture out while the sun was on this side of the planet. The driver gave them a condescending little smile and said to suit themselves. His smirk, apparently unknowing of the Geneva disaster, seemed to say, *Country vamps.*

They settled into the guest apartments (two side by side and adjoining — one for Reginald and Nikki and one for Brian) in the way they'd settle into a hotel, rested for a few hours, then took the elevator down to the main US Vampire Council floor just after dawn.

The elevator opened into a wide lobby. Nikki looked up first, then visibly flinched as she saw that the room was an atrium, complete with an unobstructed glass ceiling. Somewhere above, past the sun blocker's enormous edges, the morning sun was up. The atrium, open to the sky and dimly lit by electric lights, remained in shadow. Still, the nonchalance — the unmitigated *arrogance* — of having an uncovered atrium in a key vampire building bothered Reginald all the way down to his core. Once upon the time, this had been a human building, and the humans had wanted the sun to shine in. Leaving it in place when the building had changed ownership felt to Reginald like giving God the finger.

There was no way to skirt the atrium without feeling like fools, so they simply walked through its center, always looking up and moving quickly — at a "fast human" pace so as not to leave Reginald behind. Once they were past and in another hallway, Nikki exhaled. Brian clapped Reginald on the back and said that it was a good thing they were brothers, because if they weren't, Brian would have made his own pace and left Reginald to flop along on his own. He said it like a joke, but Reginald suspected he was being honest. Brian had a history of looking out for himself first and foremost, and the fact that Reginald warranted a slightly slower jog thorough a perfectly safe atrium (the same as Brian would have done for Talia and his kids) was strangely touching.

A guard met them halfway down the next hallway. He was dressed in a black uniform, with a Boom Stick on one hip and a human pistol on the other. He was also holding a clipboard, which he ran a finger down as they approached.

"Mr. Baskin," said the guard, looking at the clipboard. Then he looked up and met Reginald's eyes.

"Yes."

The guard looked at Brian and Nikki. Then he looked again at Brian, taking in his massiveness.

"There is no mention of guests, sir," said the guard.

"Well, I brought guests."

"It's not on the roster, sir."

Reginald put his hand on Nikki's shoulder, then spoke to the guard. "This is my wife, Nicole," he said. "And that's my brother, Brian."

There were two chrome trash cans opposite the guard. Each stood three feet tall and had a domed top with a swinging door on the front. When the guard looked at Brian, Brian walked over to the cans, picked one of them up in his massive paws, and crushed it between his palms like an accordion. Then he tucked in the edges and pressed the compacted trash can into what looked like a giant ball of aluminum foil. He did it casually, in the way most people chew gum.

"Nice to meet you," said Brian, catching the guard's eye.

The guard kept his eyes mostly on Brian, then flicked them toward Reginald. Probably subconsciously, his right hand moved toward the Boom Stick on his hip. But the idea of using it was a joke; if Brian wanted to fight the guard, he'd be able to tie him in a double knot before the man could so much as brush the handle of his weapon.

"I'm sorry," said the guard, swallowing. "I can't just let you in."

Brian reached forward. The guard flinched, but Brian was just pulling a black sharpie out of the guard's pocket. He uncapped it.

"Got a riddle for you," said Brian. He walked over to the other trash can, then drew two wide and stupid eyes on the thing above the trap door in its front. The trash can, with a door for a mouth, looked shocked. Brian pointed at it. "What is this?"

The guard looked at Nikki and Reginald, then at Brian. "Trash can?"

Brian dropped the Sharpie into his pocket, then crushed what used to be the first trash can into a tighter ball. When he'd made it more dense than should have been possible, he tossed it through the trap door of the remaining can.

"A cannibal," he said.

The guard swallowed.

"Please let us in, " Nikki purred, batting her eyelashes.

Brian reached forward, and again the guard flinched. He placed the Sharpie back in the guard's pocket, then tapped him on the head with his huge hand the way he'd tap a kid to give him an atta-boy.

"Please," he echoed in his less-sexy voice.

"S-stay right here," said the guard. He blurred through

54

a set of doors further down the hallway, then returned a moment later and waved them forward. He wrote down Brian and Nikki's full names, then told them to enjoy their stay at the Ramada, which wasn't where they were.

Once inside what turned out to be yet another hallway, Reginald, Nikki, and Brian were greeted by Charles Barkley, who tried to shake all of their hands. Nobody reciprocated, so he asked if they wanted coffee. Then he asked if they wanted one blood creamer or two in their coffees despite the fact that all three of them had declined.

Reginald gave Charles an appraising look. "Timken told you to be nice to us, didn't he?" he said.

"Hel-lo, *Charles*," Brian cooed in a sing-song voice before Charles could answer. He was wearing a smile as wide as a dinner plate. Brian had been the one member of Logan's Council that Charles had been unable to intimidate. Instead of cowering, Brian had flipped the tables on his opponent, dedicating most of his time on Council to making Charles look stupid.

"I'm just glad you agreed to help us," said Charles, the sycophantic smile falling from his lips.

"Well, threatening us will do that."

"Hel-lo *Charles*," Brian repeated.

"Did Timken threaten *you* if you didn't kiss our asses?" Reginald asked, still wondering at Charles's servility. Then he thought of something. "Wait... do you even report to Timken these days? Maybe I've got it wrong. Do you work for the esteemed Mr. Walker now?"

The idea to poke Charles with Walker had just occurred to him, but the shot clearly hit its mark. When Timken had run for the vampire presidency, Charles had been his opponent and Walker had been Charles's running mate. But in the intervening years, because Walker was better at greasing palms and licking balls than Charles,

Walker had moved above Charles. Walker was now the logical choice to replace Timken whenever Timken decided to step down, and Charles would have to pedal hard just to secure himself a job as the Secretary of Something Stupid. It had to be humiliating.

"Right this way," said Charles, avoiding Reginald's gaze. And they began walking.

"Hel-loooo *Charles*," Brian purred. He clapped a brotherly hand on Charles's back, and the impact of the gesture slammed Charles into the edge of an approaching doorway. He burst through it in an explosion of metal and plaster dust, fell to the floor covered in gypsum, and then kept walking a few paces ahead of Brian as if nothing had happened.

As they walked further, they passed a sign. It read: *American Vampire Council meeting room.* And there was an arrow pointing straight ahead.

But instead of walking into a dirt-floored arena or a chamber of monster horrors, they entered a conference room like any Reginald had seen on the human news a lifetime ago. He hadn't been to a Council meeting since the one where they'd almost been murdered and he'd only sporadically checked in on Council since the war — since more or less giving up on solving the rest of the codex. He'd known the Vampire Nation had been trending toward more and more conservative ways of operating, but the conference room's simplicity still caught him by surprise. Gone were elaborate thrones, stadium seating, and sunlight rooms meant for executions. Gone were the chains, the torturers, the sniper windows, and the long formal robes. In its place was banality, and President Nicholas Timken.

Timken was seated at the large table in the middle of the room, dressed in a conservative blue suit and a red tie.

When the group entered, he glanced briefly at Charles (who was covered in plaster dust) and then at the others. He stood, smiled warmly, and came forward.

He went to Reginald first, a broad smile on his handsome face. He took Reginald's hand in both of his, one on top and one beneath, clasping it warmly as if greeting an old friend. Reginald was almost swayed by Timken's earnest politician's eyes and his boyish surfer's hair, but then he remembered that the last time they'd met, Timken had climbed a wall, ripped a TV from its mount, and smashed it to pieces in a fit of rage. He reminded himself who Timken was back then and still was today — the man who'd spearheaded and championed the largest-scale genocide ever perpetrated. He'd done it with a straight face and a clear conscience, because something within him told him he was doing it all for the greater good, making the hard choices that nobody else had the guts to make. Which, in Reginald's mind, meant that he was deeply insane.

"Reginald," Timken said with a smile. "It's good to see you again."

Reginald kept his expression neutral. "Mr. President."

"I'm glad you're here. We need your help."

Reginald looked at Nikki, then Brian. He turned back to Timken.

"Let's make something clear," he said. "I think you're one seriously evil son of a bitch, and I am here against my will."

Timken held his gaze for a long moment, then laughed with buoyant good humor. The sound was rich and light and genuine.

"A Boy Scout to the end!" he said, smiling. "Even after all this time, you're still holding that old grudge?"

"It's a big grudge," Reginald answered.

Timken held the smile, but after a long beat his face fell and became serious. He stared at Reginald. "You still think I made the wrong decision," he said. It was a statement, not a question.

"You *did* make the wrong decision."

"You said the vampires of the world wouldn't let me make it, if I remember," said Timken.

"I did," said Reginald. "But unfortunately, *I* was the one who was wrong about that."

"Yes. Which proves that you are fallible. Come on, Reginald; you're supposed to be the logical one. Can you really say that there was zero chance you were wrong about the war?"

"Correct," he said, still holding Timken's eyes. He pulled his hand from the man's surprisingly smooth and soft grip. "Zero chance."

"Even after all this time."

"Especially after all this time. I've had forty years to regret my part in all of it, ashamed that I couldn't do more. But I see you didn't have any such conflict, and that your conscience is clear."

The president shook his head sadly. "That's why you could never lead, Reginald. You think I'm evil. That's okay, I guess; you wouldn't be the first. There are fringe groups who think I'm beyond terrible. And yes, Claude Toussant does most of the dirtiest work — I'm so sorry about your maker, by the way; I never got a chance to express my condolences — but I'll take the responsibility for those dirty jobs because it's mine in the end. I can take your accusations. But the truth is still the truth: *we are here, we are alive, and we are stronger than ever.* I would have preferred a harmonious existence with the humans too. I would have preferred to skip through meadows carrying daisies and singing songs about peaceful cooperation, but that wasn't the way it needed to be. And if I hadn't made the choice you never would have made, we wouldn't be standing here having this conversation."

"And that's a good thing?"

Timken puffed his cheeks with a burst of laughter, apparently unable to believe Reginald's statement was serious. So instead of answering what seemed to be rhetorical, he clapped Reginald on the back and motioned for them all to sit. Brian did, causing the chair to protest under his weight. Nikki sat next to Brian, and Reginald sat on Nikki's other side. Timken sat at the head of the table, behind a blotter and an attractive desk set. The desk set was comprised of two pens in holders with a tiny flag between them: blood red with an eclipsed sun in the center. Charles, brushing himself more or less clean, sat on the other side, near Timken. Then Timken pressed a button on a small intercom near the blotter and said, "You can come in now."

Both Reginald and Brian seemed to have the same thought at the same time, because they both flexed to rise. But the person Timken had summoned wasn't Claude after all. It was Ophelia Thax, the stunning general Reginald had met at Vampire World Command.

Nikki watched the men sit and compose themselves, then looked Ophelia over from her blonde head to her high-heeled black boots. She said, "You don't exactly rotate staff much around here."

Ophelia shot Nikki a look, then came to the front of the room and stood between Timken and Charles. She pressed something on the conference table and a section of the polished wood (or possibly synthetic wood, for safety) rotated upward to reveal a small screen. She began touching the screen, dimming the room's lights and bringing up a projection on the far wall. When the lights were down and the projection was up, Reginald found himself staring at a balding black man with fat cheeks covered in dark stubble.

"Walter Lafontaine," Ophelia announced, taking a small remote from the table and moving toward the projection. "Human. Known to MorningFresh Bloodworks as Stock 414-352. Twenty-nine years old. He was born at MorningFresh, then disappeared from the facility via unknown means three years ago. His mother is still stock at MorningFresh, designated 002-495. No history of disorderly conduct or defect from either stock."

"I'm sorry," said Reginald, staring at Ophelia, "but could you please refer to them as if they were people instead of property?"

"They *are* property," said Ophelia. She didn't say it with animus. She said it like a fact.

"They are *not* fucking property!" Reginald blurted, suddenly furious that he'd even come. He'd liked humans. He'd tried to save humans. He'd failed humans, and they'd all ended up being bled for a living. The casual way Ophelia was referring to them as if they were toasters suddenly felt like the last straw.

"Do you have any idea what it costs to maintain a human bloodline, especially given the losses the farms have had lately with the unexplained die-offs?" Ophelia retorted. "There is a substantial investment on behalf of MorningFresh in maintaining these assets, all of whom have been screened and assigned to breed so as to develop maximally strong, healthy bucks and fertile females who can…"

"Jesus fucking Christ!" said Reginald. "Have you seriously never read a history book?"

Ophelia looked derailed. "What?"

"Okay, I'll explain it to you. See, there was this guy

named Abraham Lincoln once upon a time. And what old Honest Abe did was…"

"There's plenty of caucasian stock too, you know," Ophelia snapped.

"That metaphor wasn't meant to be taken literally. I meant it allegorically."

"*What?*"

"And while we're talking about books," Reginald added, "have you ever seen a dictionary?"

"Look, I don't need your fucking help to…"

Timken patted the air in a pacifying gesture, cutting Ophelia off mid-sentence. Then he nodded, urging her to concede.

"Fine," she said. "Neither… *person*… has any past history of destructive or insubordinate behavior. But our reconnaissance at MorningFresh — which as you know is still locked down and under the control of insurgents — suggests that Mr. Lafontaine is the leader of a human rebellion that, through means unknown, has managed to coordinate terrorist attacks across, to date, sixteen separate locations, and…"

Reginald turned to Timken, his animosity toward the president lost to curiosity and disbelief.

"Sixteen?"

Timken nodded. "That we know of. We haven't officially released news of several events that happened somewhat quietly, but yes. They've been happening all over the globe. And it's obvious that in addition to being highly coordinated in these attacks, they've been communicating for a while. Based on some of the weapons they've developed, plus the thing with Geneva's blocker…"

"How have they been communicating?"

"We don't know," said Ophelia. "Humans in the farms are stripped of most belongings. They have their clothes and live in small shanties in the free range communities, but they're not allowed to have any technology, so it's not like they're walking around with cell phones. But somehow they all knew what to do and when to do it, and somehow they either got or made weapons. Their use of silver is especially curious. Most of it is old jewelry, but some seems to have been cobbled together from old flatware, like forks and knives and spoons. It's obviously not material that would be available in the communities."

"Serves you right for not just tying them down 24/7," said Reginald, bitterness in his voice. "Serves you right for letting them move around and have lives outside of being hooked to IV lines."

"That's what *I* told them," said Ophelia, not sensing Reginald's sarcasm.

"Anyway," said Timken, "Mr. Lafontaine here seems to be the mastermind. He released a video yesterday afternoon. He clearly has a natural flair for the dramatic, because, well…." He sighed. "Well, we'll just show you." He tipped a nod toward Ophelia, and the general pressed more buttons on the small console. The still shot of Lafontaine was replaced by a video.

Reginald saw immediately what Timken had been talking about. The video, which showed Lafontaine sitting in what was clearly a cave, reminded Reginald of terrorist videos he'd grown up seeing on the human news from the likes of Osama Bin Laden. There was even a hooded figure in a chair beside him, wrapped in silver. Lafontaine was wearing sunglasses, as if he got what Osama had been going for, but thought he could cool it up a little.

Lafontaine stood and began to circle. As the camera pulled back, Reginald got a better look at the supposed human mastermind — and when it did, the man began to look less and less like a traditional terrorist. Lafontaine was carrying a fair amount of weight, somehow sporting a gut out in the wildlands at the end of the world. Yet, despite his heavy frame, Reginald saw that the man was much more limber and agile than he himself ever had been as a human. Lafontaine moved with impatient energy, walking and talking as if time were short.

"This is the beginning of your end," he told the camera. "By the time you see this, we will have seized several of your farms and at least one of your biggest cities." He walked over and pulled the hood from the silver-wrapped vampire who, Reginald realized, was wearing a CPC uniform. The officer spat and snarled the minute his hood was removed.

Lafontaine continued. "You have kept us in cages. You have taken our blood. You have taken our *planet*. So we have taken a few of your people. We know what hurts you. We know what doesn't." He gave a disturbing little smile. "And we have something new to show you."

Someone off-camera handed Lafontaine a syringe. Lafontaine stabbed the syringe into the vampire's arm, and the CPC officer immediately began to writhe and thrash as if whatever was in the syringe burned. His fangs descended; he started to snap at the black man like an angry snake. Keeping away from his prisoner's mouth, Lafontaine pulled up the vampire's sleeve to expose the point of injection. The camera moved closer. The pale vampire's skin was black in one spot like a bruise, but the blackness was already visibly spreading.

"Back in the war, the human troops had a weapon," he said. "They put it in bullets. We took it out of those bullets and we made it better." His face twisted in cruel, remorseless anger. "We made it much, *much* better, and we put it back into bullets." Then he paused and made a small, vengeful smile. "Oh, and we also put it in other things — things that are much *bigger* than bullets."

Behind him, the vampire's skin crawled with darkness, the bruise now the size of a grapefruit. Ophelia pressed a button and the video paused. The vampire's mouth froze open in pain, his fangs down.

Timken shook his head. "Animal."

Brian's head snapped toward the president. With his vampire's speed, it looked like a jump cut in a film, as if his head had suddenly been swapped between frames.

"Really," he said.

"I could let you watch the rest of the video," said Timken. "They recorded the entire thing. It takes over an hour for the man to die. Most of it is just screaming."

"I seem to remember you vowing to eliminate 99 percent of the human population," said Reginald. "I'd argue that makes you *almost* as much of an animal as this guy who killed one vampire."

"I never did anything with malice," said Timken, his eyes becoming annoyed.

"Well, that makes it better," said Nikki.

Ophelia flipped the video off, then put the still of Lafontaine back on the screen. "The vampire's name was Calvin Gregory," she said. "He was stationed just outside New York, on patrol in wildlands, so we're assuming the video was taken nearby. That looks like a cave he's in, but I don't know of any natural caves outside of New York. Our guess it that it's something they hollowed out below ground. But that raises all sorts of questions, the most obvious of which is, *How?* It'd have to be dug out with machinery, so why didn't we see it happen on the satellites? How did nobody hear it? And how did they reinforce the cave once they'd made it? It'd take materials and knowledge they shouldn't have access to."

Reginald shrugged. "Humans are resourceful. Don't you remember?"

Timken laughed. "Humans weren't as resourceful back when Ophelia was one."

"We…"

But as soon as he'd begun speaking, Reginald stopped himself. Despite the fact that he'd been a vampire longer than he'd been a human, he'd just referred to himself as the wrong species. He started again.

"*They* have a tendency to find a way if you give them half a chance. You killed most of their population, but you didn't go around and burn the planet. Vampires took a lot of the obvious conveniences and technology, but there's a lot of world still out there that you never touched. All those houses with all those supplies in them? The humans have obviously scavenged better and figured out more than you gave them credit for." Then he thought of Lafontaine's gut and added, "They're even eating well."

Ophelia shook her head. "How?" she said, clearly dumbfounded. Despite being military, Reginald had noticed that the general had a big blind spot in her ability to reason. She'd underestimated her opponents for so long — and had mistakenly relegated them to the intelligence and docility of sheep — that their biting back was almost offensive to her worldview.

Reginald shrugged. "Canned foods. Twinkies. I don't know, and the details are irrelevant. But what's key here is that you aren't *considering* some of the more obvious questions."

"Like what?"

"Well, how was that video recorded?"

Ophelia looked at Timken. "We could figure it out. I'll get back to you."

"It doesn't matter. But whatever they took it with required power. So how are they generating power?"

Again, Timken and Ophelia looked at each other.

Reginald shook his head. His brain was operating faster and faster, plans and strategies and permutations beginning to string together like the inevitable series of actions in a clockwork mousetrap. Unlike in the war, the vampire power structures weren't remotely prepared for any of this. They didn't understand what they were facing because they were willfully blind, having never considered it possible. It made them so vulnerable as to be laughable.

"You're like people who've decided to shoot down a plane with a slingshot," said Reginald. "I don't know where to begin to tell you what to do because you're not capable of knowing the right questions to ask. You're going to ask me how to build a bigger slingshot, but the slingshot isn't the answer and never has been. Your entire premise is flawed from end to end."

Ophelia stared at him, insulted.

Reginald raised a hand, ticking off points on his fingers as he spoke. "You don't know where they are, and that's just this one community. You don't know how they've been communicating, which it's clear they've been doing nearly in real time. You don't know how they hacked the Geneva sun blocker. You don't know how they got the silver or the weapons — were those things sneaked in, or were they somehow made on-site? But even that is just the tip of the iceberg. The bigger problem is what you don't know you don't know. For instance: if they could sabotage the sun blocker, what's to say they couldn't breach a major city's gates? You've only left one major entrance in each city, because hey, we're the top dogs! No need to worry about the wild humans or have a Plan B, because they're just animals, right?" He shook his head. "You don't know what kind of weapons they might have. They seem to have dug up some of the old AVT rifles, if they got to the AVT's bullets. So did they just strip dead soldiers for old weapons, or did they build new weapons? And if so, what will those new weapons do, and can they make more of them? Are they training assault groups? Armies, maybe? Did you figure out where the major AVT deployments were, and hence where they might have found the bio agent they seem to have made deadlier over the years? Did you even look?"

"We just assumed..." Ophelia began.

Reginald shook his head. "You've *always* assumed. Do you know the story of how I first escaped from the Vampire Council? Nikki here helped me. They *assumed* she was a vampire because she acted like one and flashed some fake fangs at them, and so they tried to execute her like one. They *assumed* I'd either futilely fight back on my own or let myself be killed, not that I might think of a third strategy they'd never considered." He scooted back in his chair, crossed one leg over the other. "Well, now you've *assumed* that because the contingents of AVT soldiers were gone, that the human threat to you was gone. You left all of that land out there, with whatever rich deposits of goodies were waiting to be found. Or maybe not even *found*; maybe the humans have always had bunkers filled with smart people and smart weapons. Maybe they've just been biding their time, multiplying in number out of sight, and making those good weapons better. Like the weapon they used to have in those gray bullets." Reginald put a hand on his chest. "Now, I know I watched a vampire take all day to die from some sort of a biological weapon during the war. So if *I*, as a regular Joe, saw that, then obviously *you* smart leader types saw it too, and of course you investigated and found out exactly what that weapon was, and how to protect us against it in the future." He looked mildly at Timken and Ophelia, who looked slapped. When they didn't react, he shook his head and continued, almost sadly. "But of course you didn't, did you? Because you're *vampires*. And you're on the *top* of the food chain."

Something shifted inside of Ophelia. Reginald watched her hard expression soften for the first time since he'd first met her under the ice in Antarctica. He could tell it was killing her to drop her sense of superiority, but she seemed to have realized that she was no longer entirely superior... and that maybe she'd never actually been in control.

"That's why we need your help," she said. She swallowed at the last word, seeming to have forced it out.

Reginald let himself smirk. "Okay. You want help? Here's my advice: bunker in. Get the people you care about and dig yourself a hole. Because this is what I've been talking about from the beginning, and you never listened."

Timken looked over. "The apocalypse again."

"Yes. Again." He rolled his eyes, shaking his head. "You fucking people," he said. "Ever since my first year, vampires have been coming to me and asking me to tell them what to do. People acted like I was oracle even before I'd heard of the vampire codex. But if I'm this big, perfect computer mind — which is the way people act when I'm asked for help — then why don't you listen to what that big computer mind tells you? I told you forty years ago that this was coming."

Timken's composure broke. He'd finally had enough civility. He stood.

"Yes, Reginald! Forty years ago! And it never happened! We built a whole society in that time! We were right, not you!"

"You were right? But isn't that the biggest assumption of

all?" Reginald stood to match the president, then waved his arms theatrically overhead as if beckoning toward the heavens. "If you were right, where are the angels? Why haven't they returned to pat you on the back and tell you that you done good?"

Timken chuckled humorlessly. "I think with angels, no news is good news."

Reginald shook his head and said nothing. His eyes rolled toward the projection at the front of the room, then toward Timken.

"This is not the apocalypse!" Timken yelled. Then he composed himself, smoothing his hair. "This is just one lunatic, who's…"

"Who's managed to put together a string of events across the entire planet and coordinated a group of people who supposedly have no access to technology, no power, no food…"

"Isolated incidents!"

"SIXTEEN INCIDENTS!" Reginald boomed. He wasn't used to anger, and even after nearly eighty years on the planet, he certainly wasn't used to squaring off in a verbal fight. It had always been his way to demure and let the other person win, but he'd had enough. The stupidity here was too thick. They'd either listen or let them go home. There was no third choice.

Timken looked over at Ophelia, who hadn't moved. She gave a small shrug. Timken returned to his chair but didn't sit, standing over it with his hands on the table like a vulture.

"Fine. Let's say you're right."

"The codex is right."

"Whatever. So why has it taken so long?"

"Maybe they had to swell their numbers. Maybe they needed time to develop their weapons. Or maybe they just needed time to get pissed off enough. To find time to believe."

Timken sat. When he spoke, he sounded defeated.

"Okay, Reginald. Humans are going to rise up. They're on a holy mission. Whatever. So what do we do?"

"Nothing. In the words of some angels I once knew, 'You're fucked.'"

"Oh, that's helpful," said Charles, who'd been surprisingly quiet throughout the whole briefing. Reginald had almost forgotten he was there, still covered in white drywall dust.

"Look," said Reginald. "I don't know what you expect from me. You threatened me to get me here, so I'm here. But if I give you advice, I think we all know you aren't going to take it. So... just tell me what you want to do and I'll tell you to go ahead and do it. We can all pretend this worked out the way we wanted." He looked into Timken's eyes. "So just tell me, Mr. President: what do you want me to do?"

Timken looked at Reginald, then plucked an invisible piece of dust from his lapel. "Lafontaine made one demand at the end of the video," he said. "Help us meet that demand as best you can, and you can go."

Reginald sighed. "What does he want?"

Timken once again exchanged a glance with the general. "He wants to meet," he said.

SIX

Fatass

"Put it there."

"It doesn't fit."

"Turn it, fatass."

Reginald, deep down inside his own mind, put his mental hands on his fat mental hips and stared at the nonexistent teenager in front of him, kneeling beside the imaginary puzzle. He wondered what it said about his self esteem that even in the privacy of his own mind, he was insulting himself.

"Don't call me 'fatass,'" said Reginald's mental projection of Reginald.

"Don't blame me, fatass," said Reginald's mental projection of Maurice. "I'm not actually here."

It was true. Maurice wasn't actually there any more than the gigantic floor puzzle in front of them was there. "Maurice" was just Reginald's way of projecting his maker's blood memories into a visual that made sense while he was inside his own headspace. "Maurice" had all of the real Maurice's memories, quirks, and tendencies, but everything he did these days was really just another facet of Reginald. It was tempting to pretend that Maurice was still here and alive in a way, but down that road was madness. When Reginald had first discovered the ability to bloodwalk (which the angel Balestro had given him for a reason Reginald still didn't understand), Reginald remembered being entranced with the idea of becoming lost down here, walking through the vampire family tree forever, putting his various ancestors on like so many gloves. But the family tree within him was just like the codex, which Reginald had currently chosen to represent as a floor puzzle: it was just an archive, and nothing more. Pretending a life could be lived in it would have been as close to death as a vampire could get without disintegrating into ash.

"Well, then stop insulting me, Reginald," said Reginald.

Maurice (who wasn't actually Maurice, Reginald reminded himself) was still down on his hands and knees, studying the puzzle. He turned his head toward Reginald. Reginald knelt beside him, then took a piece of the puzzle in his hands. He turned it one way, then another. Eventually he slipped it into place. At the same moment, he felt a tiny jolt inside of his real mind as another little thing, unseen and distant, somehow made sense. The sensation felt good, and being with "Maurice" again felt good as well. It made him forget why he'd neglected the puzzle and his blood memories in the first place. But then he remembered why — and remembered what circumstances had set him to work on it again now — and some of the pleasure faded back away.

In the way you can recognize the picture on a puzzle before it's finished, Reginald had known the codex's broad strokes since he'd first begun to piece it together forty years ago. It foretold the human revolution, but didn't dwell much on the vampire revolution other than to say that the latter had made the former possible. He could read a few other things from the in-progress puzzle as well — most notably that humans, not vampires, were considered by the angels to be the stronger species. The humans had always had the power to eradicate the world's vampires, but they hadn't realized it until they'd been *forced* to realize it by the decimation of their population — which had forced them to evolve, and made them desperate enough to strike.

But because Reginald had let the puzzle lay fallow for so long, there were vast areas of it that were still unsolved — foggy places where Reginald could only guess at the gaps in his knowledge. He couldn't tell where the codex's prophecies ended, for instance. But sometimes it almost looked as if the human revolution was the final event the puzzle predicted, and that filled Reginald with dread. The codex was the pre-told history of vampirekind. If it ended with the human revolution, what did that say about their chances of surviving?

"Maurice?" said Reginald. He knew that Maurice wasn't really there and that he was just talking to himself, but talking to oneself had its uses.

"Yes, Reginald."

"If this is all inevitable —" He gestured out across the vast puzzle, which in Reginald's mind's eye stretched to the horizon. "— then why am I bothering to help Timken? Should we just run?"

"If you run," said Maurice, slotting another piece into the puzzle, "then they'll kill you."

"We're all doomed anyway. Or so the codex says."

"That's not what the codex says."

"So the codex implies, then," said Reginald.

Mental Maurice turned to look at him again. "Since when were you a slave to rules?"

Reginald thought about it — a thought within his current state of thought. It was true. Reginald wasn't a punk rocker or a rebel, but he'd never considered societal norms to have much merit. Human rules said that people were more or less equal and should be treated as equals, but everyone had always mocked Reginald for being fat. Vampire rules said that inferior vampires shouldn't be allowed to live, and he'd lived despite being considered inferior. But even that was a set of nested dolls, because he *wasn't* inferior, despite being *considered* inferior. The way in which people kept asking him for advice (before ignoring it because they, who were clearly *not* inferior, knew better) proved that he was considered superior at least some of the time. So what did all those rules really mean in the end?

"But this is all, like, predestined," said Reginald.

"More or less. But look at how there's always been wiggle room. You remember what I said, right? About how angels don't understand free will?"

"Then how could *any* of this have been predestined, if there's all this free will?"

"That's not what I said, fatass," said Maurice.

Reginald wondered if the stickiness of his current predicament was the reason he was so intent on insulting himself through Maurice, but ultimately it didn't matter. He and Mental Maurice had had this discussion over and over and over again, Reginald versus Reginald, trying to riddle out one of the greatest philosophical riddles of all time: was it possible to have both choice and destiny? Could one system incorporate the other?

Reginald just shook his head. He plucked another piece of information from the memory of a vampire who'd lived and died four millennia earlier, then set it next to a casual interaction that Maurice himself had observed just fifty years ago. The two pieces fit and leant meaning to each other. Reginald felt a small realization, then kept working.

"It's interesting," said Reginald.

Maurice just looked over. Because he was Maurice's memories animated by Reginald's thought processes, he already knew what Reginald found interesting. But to keep the back and forth going, he said, "What is?"

"We aren't actually immortal."

Maurice smiled. It was the real Maurice smiling. Reginald could feel the difference. Maurice's blood ran through Reginald's veins, and vampire blood had a sort of consciousness of its own. He'd never talk to Maurice for real again, but this was the sort of thing that Maurice would have agreed with, and found clever.

"It *is* interesting, isn't it?" said Maurice.

"Why do you think we always end up dying in the end?"

Maurice shrugged. "As the great sage Chuck Palahniuk once said, 'On a long enough timeline, the survival rate for everyone drops to zero.' Nothing lives forever. Immortality is about potential, not reality. There are one-celled organisms that can live forever, but their immortality assumes that the people watching out for them give them everything they need to keep living, and that they don't eventually just get bored and throw those organisms into the incinerator. We have the biological *potential* to live forever, but literally doing so is impossible."

"Why?"

"Because forever is forever. It's never over, so nobody can ever get there. The best you can do is 'immortal… so far.'"

"Very philosophical," said Reginald.

Maurice looked back to the puzzle and resumed sorting pieces. "Besides, the odds just aren't in immortality's favor.

Not as it exists for vampires, anyway. It's pretty unlikely that you'd ever just wake up one day and walk into a sharp stake, but it's possible, right? So if it's possible, it'll eventually happen in the true sense of forever, given infinite chances. Same with being attacked by a random crazy person, or being decapitated in an accident. What happens when the sun one day swells and its corona burns Earth to a cinder? What then? Or what if you simply decide one day that you've had enough of living, and walk out into the sun?"

Reginald looked at the Maurice who wasn't really Maurice, realizing all at once how much he missed him.

"Had you had enough of living, Maurice?" he asked.

Maurice gave him a tight-lipped frown. Reginald knew what the expression meant: that Maurice was just an echo, and that he couldn't actually answer the question in the here and now.

"Just make a guess," said Reginald.

"I'd lived for over two thousand years, Reginald," Maurice's memories told him. "I doubt I actually *wanted* to die, but the fact that I did isn't a tragedy. Claude didn't end a life that wouldn't, one day, have ended anyway."

"So because we all die in the end, nothing is worthwhile," said Reginald.

Maurice shook his head — a gesture that was totally and completely Maurice. "Don't be such a nihilist, fatass," he said.

Reginald looked at the vast puzzle, then nodded to Maurice. Maurice nodded back. The exchange of nods declared that progress on the codex's assembly had been made, so Reginald let the fog dissipate and withdrew from his headspace. A moment later he resurfaced in his room in the USVC building, where Nikki was sitting beside him, clicking away on her laptop. He sat up and looked at the screen. She was perusing Fangbook, checking in on her various groups.

"You're awake," she said.

"I wasn't asleep."

"Were you working on the codex?"

"Mmm-hmm."

"Was it rusty? Did you have a hard time getting back in?"

"Not at all. It actually felt good to put my mental hands back to work. Comfortable, even."

Her eyes softened. "Was Maurice still there?"

Reginald sighed. "I don't think its healthy for either of us to think of him as if he were a person," he said. Then he caught his slip and corrected himself: "… to think of *it* as if *it* were a person."

He rolled to the side and cupped Nikki's calf with his hand. She was wearing the robe provided by the building's domestic housekeeping staff, just like maid service in a hotel. The robe was unsexy, but Nikki made it work.

"Did you figure out what's up with Timken?" she asked.

Reginald consulted what he'd seen in his head: the slightly-more-assembled codex and the emotional readings he'd gotten from Timken during the meeting. Timken, like Claude, had seemed to know that he should keep his mental shutters up around the Chosen One, but Reginald had still gotten the flavor of his thoughts — enough to proceed and not run off screaming, anyway.

"He's being honest with us. Timken isn't a problem. Claude is the problem, and if he's smart, he'll stay away."

"Like Walker," said Nikki. They'd already laughed about Walker's absence in the meeting. Nikki had said she resented his not being there. She wanted to knee him in the testicles. Reginald had assured her that it still hurt a vampire man when his boys got crushed.

"The thing about Timken is that he's always believed he's doing the right thing," said Reginald. "That's what's so terrible about him. It's almost hard to hate him because he's always trying; he just tries in such horrible ways. He's like a Boy Scout in spirit, but he doesn't realize he's looking at life through a melted piece of glass."

"Mmm."

"So, fine," said Reginald with a sigh. "We'll help them set up their meeting with Lafontaine. Try to keep Timken from being killed. And if…"

Nikki raised her eyebrows at him.

"Hey, I don't want Timken killed. Not now."

Nikki raised her eyebrows further.

"The cows have left the barn, my darling. Humanity got a pole up the ass already. All that would happen if Timken died now would be Walker, Claude, or Charles stepping in. It's time we talk about the least of all assholes."

"Wow," said Nikki. "You're right. How terrible."

"Hey," said Reginald, rolling onto his back, "that's politics for you."

There was a knock on the door. Reginald answered it while Nikki closed her laptop and set it aside. He found Ophelia in the hallway, with Brian already dressed and ready beside her. Brian nodded, apparently to let Reginald know that everything appeared to be more or less under control. It was a ludicrous gesture, but it was totally Brian. He was assuring Reginald that it would be okay to listen to Ophelia, because he could take her down if she got ornery. It was true, but it was stupid.

"We're ready," said Ophelia.

Reginald turned to Nikki. She stood and began walking toward her suitcase.

"Five minutes," said Reginald as Nikki slipped the robe from her shoulders.

He closed the door. Brian, who'd been peering through the closing door and watching Nikki's bare back, said, "Dammit."

SEVEN

Mental

On the walk down to what Reginald assumed would be
some sort of a situation room, Ophelia gave them an
update. Reginald had gone to sleep immediately after
returning from their previous meeting, then had gone into
his codex trance immediately after waking. Nikki had been
surfing Fangbook, but most of what Ophelia had to report
wasn't public anyway.

"There have been two new incidents," she told them.
"One happened just outside New York at another blood
farm… and this despite the fact that all of the farms were
cautioned to be on high alert." She shook her head.
"Idiots. Somehow the stock still got the best of the guards.
We don't know how. We don't know if the insurgents were
on milkers at the time or locked down in their cells; it's not
a free-range facility. We also have no idea what they're
using for weapons, except that as in the other incursions,
they're using silver for restraint. What's going on there is
totally inside the walls and the public is unaware. The only
reason we even know there *was* an incident is because they
told us about it."

Reginald looked over at Ophelia, trying to keep up with her brisk pace. "They?"

"The humans at the facility. One of them got a phone from one of the guards, took video, and emailed it to us."

"Here? Directly to the USVC?"

Ophelia nodded grimly. "The president's classified personal email account. We have no idea how they got the address." She walked faster. "The other incident was an electronic incursion on Fangbook. A hack. It…"

Nikki interrupted. "I didn't see anything on Fangbook," she said.

"They didn't get far. Fangbook is almost as tight as the USVC itself, with the exception of email, apparently. We use Fangbook as a redundant information archive. Keep that under your hat, though; vampires don't like to think that the government is harvesting their information. But it's good that we were, because that's how we spotted the hack while it was still in progress."

"Did you trace it?" said Reginald.

Ophelia said nothing and kept walking.

Reginald laughed. "I guess not. Pretty good for a bunch of monkeys, huh? So that means the incident with the Geneva sun blocker *was* a hack. So not only can they bust your security, but you have no idea how they're doing it, where they're doing it from, or where they're getting equipment that can go toe-to-toe with yours. Or how they've gotten the minds together to figure all of this out in the first place."

He looked at Ophelia's face as they walked. She seemed vaguely angry, but it was a helpless sort of anger. She mostly looked as if she just wanted it all to go away, and for Reginald to stop talking about it.

"Oh, but that's not even the whole story, is it?" he said, now chuckling openly while reading her face. "You've done a bunch of futile satellite surveys, haven't you? Because you've figured out that all of this would take a lab — a *big* lab, probably the size of a small city. Because those humans have got a lot to do, right? They're developing new weapons, creating biological warfare agents, probably hotwiring computers and chips. And that last one is a hell of a task in itself, because given all of the technological advances the vampire government must have had in the past forty years, the humans would need to have some seriously impressive computers if they hoped to even keep up with…"

Reginald stopped because he'd caught a flitting thought from Ophelia's mind while simultaneously reading a pained expression on her face. The one-two punch of realizations made him burst into rich laughter.

"You haven't *had* any advances!" he blurted. The thought was so funny that he stumbled sideways into Brian. "You haven't! You kept making new computers based on the old models, and you piggybacked on the human internet, and you figured out how to use the humans' resources to launch and build the space stations behind the sun blockers. But you haven't *changed* them at all, have you? You've just copied their work, without ever making any improvements!"

Ophelia said nothing and walked faster. Reginald followed behind, feeling strangely vindicated. Something had clicked in his mind, and he felt a handful of pieces of the codex fall into place without effort. He'd known since the end of the war that there was a strong link between the human and vampire species, but he'd never worked out the nature of that link. Now, watching Ophelia, he realized that what the angels had said all those years ago was true: that vampires simply weren't any good at evolving. When he'd first heard Santos say that in the angels' anteroom back in Luxembourg, he'd assumed it was a comment on their society — that vampires were so arrogant and complacent that they were content to sit on their laurels, never becoming more than they already were. But now he saw that the truth might be more literal, and that mental improvement might actually be beyond vampires other than himself. Was it possible that what was true of vampire bodies was true of vampire minds as well? Over the course of centuries, Reginald knew he could maximize the limited potential he'd been given and achieve speed and strength relative to humans, but he'd never be able to lose weight or surpass the strength of a vampire currently stronger than him. Was that also true of thought? Were the world's vampires frozen with a set amount of intelligence at the time of turning and incapable of truly evolving and innovating?

Reginald was still laughing. Brian and Nikki didn't seem to appreciate the joke (or get it; they had vampire minds, after all, har-har) and stared at him as his eyes started to water. But Reginald found the situation hilarious. *Hilaaaaaarious.* Here they were, forty years down the road, and nothing had changed. The population looked exactly the same, and they were all still using the same technology — not just in the cities, but all the way at the top, in the military and government. The world had hit a stand-still. Perusing vampire history in the absence of human innovation was like reading the same page of a book over and over again.

"Well, hell," said Reginald, wiping his eyes. "*That's* your problem. They're pressing buttons while you're sharpening sticks and wondering why the moon runs away every month. Oh, you are *soooo* fucked."

But beneath the laughter, as it dissipated, Reginald felt himself sober. This had been going on for forty years. *Forty*

years. If the humans had evolved while vampires had stag-
nated, what surprises might they have in store after *forty
fucking years?*

They made their way to a room in what seemed to be
the basement of the building. Then, after Reginald
promised to stop mocking Ophelia and their entire race,
she gave them updates on the existing incidents.

They'd heard from ambassador Karl Stromm in
Geneva. Karl reported that the EU Council had finally
gotten back on its feet after the sun blocker incident, in
which over five hundred vampires had burned to death.
Geneva had gotten used to working 24 hours a day, but the
city had once been unblocked like every other city besides
New York, and it still had tunnels and tube walkways
between most of the important buildings. (They did not,
however, have many shielded cars in the city, having
deemed them unnecessary. Reginald had to fight not to
laugh when he heard it.) Most of the actual Council had
survived and was back at work in the way most cities
handled business: operating mainly at night, keeping to
one location during the day.

There were also some reports of the biological weapon
Lafontaine had demonstrated in his video. All of the insti-
tutions that had been under siege were still under siege,
and several times a sole guard or worker had been released
at night, then run screaming for the fences. In each case,
the vampire had been discovered with a strange black
gunshot wound that wouldn't heal, and in each case the
vampire had been dead within an hour. Rumors of these
incidents were beginning to filter onto Fangbook, and
several news outlets had gotten footage of the wounds
while covering the human-controlled facilities. A
simmering sense of panic was starting to brew.

As he listened to the reports, Reginald's jocularity

turned to frustration. He wasn't sure whose side he was on — human or vampire — because both sides were wrong. The two species *could* coexist; they'd done so for millennia with humans mostly being none the wiser. When he and Nikki had been young before the war, they'd always "sipped and shipped," taking only enough blood from the humans they fed on to nourish themselves and then glamouring the humans into forgetfulness. Yes, they had been parasites, but they had been relatively harmless as far as parasites go. Fewer and fewer vampires had found killing their prey acceptable, if for no other reason other than that improved human police procedures made murder difficult to get away with. And of course, adding in what he'd recently realized, Reginald mentally added that vampire evasion would never keep up with those improved human procedures, because vampires didn't innovate.

But the failure of innovation would lead to dire consequences here and now, too, and Ophelia seemed to be blind to them. Vampire scientists — if there were such things — wouldn't be able to crack the human biological weapon unless they managed a peek at the humans' secret recipe, and they certainly wouldn't be able to formulate a defense. How could they? Reginald had learned early on that nobody even understood the so-called "agent" that made them vampires. Vampires weren't curious. They didn't explore or ask questions. Vampires simply *became…* and then they *were.*

Humanity had discovered a loophole. They couldn't physically outmatch vampires, but they hadn't been able to physically outmatch mammoths or saber-toothed tigers, either. The strongest muscle on planet Earth had always been the one between a human's soft, fragile ears.

The vampire codex's prediction of a human victory — and subsequent extermination of the entire vampire population — was beginning to seem inevitable by the time Reginald, Nikki, Brian, and Ophelia reached the ready room in the basement, but Reginald still had to try — starting with being maximally prepared for Timken's meeting with the human leader. He looked over all of the intel on Lafontaine, the human resistance network (most of what they knew was what the humans had shown them in their now-eighteen incidents of sabotage and insurgence), and the location that Lafontaine had proposed meeting. The soldiers who would supervise the meeting armed themselves — first with armor and the Freddy Kruger claws Reginald had first seen in use by V-Crews, then reluctantly with sidearms and assault rifles. This was a contested point amongst the proud soldiers, but Reginald, who still didn't know which side he was on, insisted. Humans were vulnerable to bullets, so the vampires should carry bullets. A spray of machine gun fire could still do things that a vampire couldn't.

Several times during the briefing and preparation, Reginald caught himself second-guessing his own words and actions. There was no way to win. He didn't want to help Timken (and, by extension, Claude — Maurice's brother and murderer), and he didn't want to kill humans. But he also didn't want to be exterminated, and he didn't want Nikki, Brian, or any of the world's innocents to die from a cruel and painful weaponized virus. Even during the height of the war, there had been many vampires who had sat idly by, hiding in their basements and praying for conflict to pass over them. There were many who took no sides, and many who were complicit without actually doing any killing themselves. Today, that number had swelled. Before the war, there had been seventy thousand vampires in the world, and most of them had been hardened by years as hunters and killers, most having self-selected to train and then become creatures of the night. Today's vampires were powder puffs by comparison. Many had been turned against their will to swell the vampire population, or had turned voluntarily because they preferred it to death or slavery. Modern vampires had tried to adapt their old human surroundings to their new natures instead of learning how to be vampires. They didn't know how to hunt, how to fight, or even how to feed from anything beyond a blood pouch. As much as Reginald hated vampirekind, he couldn't bring himself to hate most of the individuals who comprised it. They were simply too sad to loathe.

So they armed and they planned. It was all they could do, unless they wanted to wait to be eradicated by default.

Ophelia gave them bulletins as the time leading up to the meeting drained away: vampire populations in large cities looting stores, vampires rioting for vengeance, hippies clamoring for understanding and the cessation of hostilities, yelling that two wrongs didn't make a right. At the sites of at least three demonstrations, the two sides clashed, leading to bloodshed, and buildings burned.

Eventually the time to depart arrived. Reginald and Timken climbed into an armored Lincoln Town Car and the soldiers loaded into an old human SWAT vehicle wearing armor much like Timken's SA used to wear, save the bright red helmets. Then, with the car in front and the SWAT truck well behind, they made their way to an abandoned utility warehouse in the middle of a rolling section of upstate New York. The SWAT truck fell back while the car headed to the station, parked, and waited.

A short while later, a similar black car arrived and parked twenty yards away. Reginald told the two guards who'd ridden with them to keep their weapons down and their teeth in check, then advanced halfway with Timken at his side. The other car's doors opened and Lafontaine stepped out, flanked by two guards. The guards were armored. Each was holding a weapon similar to the ones Reginald had seen the AVT use in the war, now stream-lined and somehow different. Then, as the two guards remained rooted, Lafontaine advanced alone, into the space between the two parties.

When he was fifteen feet from Reginald and Timken, Lafontaine gestured toward the door of the warehouse. Reginald had already sent a crew to check the building for traps, and while the crew had been checking it out, they'd reported seeing humans on the horizon, watching through (and here, they'd laughed) binoculars. But Reginald, who didn't laugh in reply, was sure they'd also be watching through the scopes of rifles filled with gray bullets.

They walked in.

Outside, the humans crested the hill. The vampire soldiers arrived on foot. And the two species began to cover the area like a swarm of locusts.

EIGHT

Sit-Down

Both the guards and Lafontaine — tall, overweight, balding, seemingly in his thirties despite records that placed him in his twenties — were wearing mirrored sunglasses in spite of the darkness. Reginald's vampire eyes could usually see through mirroring, but he couldn't see through Lafontaine's glasses at all. They weren't normal sunglasses. They had to be another human innovation, intended to keep things on the level and to keep the two vampires from meeting his eyes.

There was a simple card table (plastic, not wood) in the middle of the room. On each side of the table was one folding metal chair. Timken sat in one and Lafontaine, with a glance at Reginald, sat in the other. Reginald stood beside the card table, feeling like a waiter.

"You were supposed to come alone," said Lafontaine.

"You'll be glad he's here," said Timken. "Reginald is the best mind we have."

Lafontaine glanced at him again. "That's exactly why I'm *not* glad he's here."

"This was the only way it made sense." Timken

shrugged good-naturedly. "I'm just a figurehead. He's our best negotiator. Not that I want him to bamboozle you, you understand. Just that we owe it to everyone to have the best minds on this."

Lafontaine took a third look at Reginald, but this time he looked him over very slowly, starting at his feet and working his way upward. He spent a lot of time on Reginald's face, trying to read him. The only other place he lingered nearly as long was Reginald's huge gut.

Finally he turned his head, with its sparse hair, toward Timken. "Did you just say 'bamboozle'?"

"You know what I mean. I just mean we're not trying to trick you."

"I know what it means. It just doesn't sound like something a vampire would say." He glanced yet again toward Reginald. "Are you two really vampires?"

"I could drink your blood if you'd like," said Reginald.

Lafontaine stared directly at him, his mirrored lenses locked on Reginald's eyes. Reginald had extended his fangs, but he was wielding them in the least threatening way possible. He was standing beside the table with his two white teeth resting over his lower lip and wearing a nonplussed expression on his face. Given the look, he'd only have been threatening to a buffet.

The tension broke, and Lafontaine laughed. Reginald retracted his fangs.

"Should it bother me, that there are two of you and only one of me?" said the human.

"No," said Reginald. "Seeing as you still have us by the balls."

Timken shot him a look. It was never good practice, in a negotiation, to admit to being at a loss, but Reginald could read the human like a book despite their lack of eye contact. Lafontaine had come into this negotiation equally arrogant and desperate — a combination that came off to Reginald like Napoleon as a suicide bomber. Neither Lafontaine nor humanity as a whole had anything to lose beyond what they'd already lost. They couldn't intimidate Lafontaine and they couldn't bulldoze through him, so the only way to lower his guard was to concede, roll over, and expose their bellies. It would be the last thing the leader of a human insurgence would expect from vampires.

Lafontaine nodded, smiling slightly. "That we do."

"What do you want?" said Timken. This time, Reginald was the one who shot a look. They hadn't exchanged enough pleasantries. Timken was a seasoned politician and knew better than to barge on so bullheadedly. But Reginald could feel his mood, and what he felt was interesting: the vampire president was nervous.

"Freedom."

"You're free," said Timken. "I'm told you escaped years ago."

"I did. But I want freedom for all humans."

Timken shook his head. "We need blood. That's not negotiable, seeing as we can't survive without it."

"And we have our fingers on your key factories," said Lafontaine. "You play ball and we'll maybe work something out. But if you won't, we'll burn them."

"We can rebuild. And the humans inside them now will never make it out alive."

Lafontaine shifted in his chair. "Mister President, let me ask you a question," he said. "Would you want to keep living if your life consisted of waiting to be bled?"

Timken shook his head — not to say that he wouldn't want a life of bleeding, but in exasperation. "No deal," he said. "Lay down your arms, and maybe we'll let some of you live."

Reginald looked again at Timken. Now he was being

aggressive — a strange breed of aggression that Reginald could feel being born out of fear. He wondered again at Timken's behavior. The president shouldn't be nervous. He'd once staged a violent coup on the American Vampire Council. He'd gotten into bed with the murderous head of the Annihilist Faction and been at least half responsible for the ending of seven billion lives. He'd led the USVC for forty years, through the worst turmoil the world had ever seen. So why was he nervous now?

The script Reginald had laid out was straightforward. Lafontaine would ask for the liberation of all of the blood farms, and Timken would counteroffer by giving him two of them. It would be enough to pacify the humans into at least a partial stand-down, and they could handle the loose ends later. Reginald had arranged to have the soldiers at the ready, in two concentric rings. The soldiers would protect their exit if the negotiations went as planned, or be prepared for an extraction if something went wrong. But Timken wasn't giving in. He wasn't apologizing on behalf of his people for the humans' treatment. He wasn't giving the human resistance leader the nuggets that he was supposed to, that he could take back to his followers as trophies of victory. Reginald tried to probe him, but he couldn't get any thoughts at all from Timken despite beginning to push. He could only get moods, meaning that Timken was deliberately keeping Reginald out.

Lafontaine leaned back and crossed his arms over his chest. It was almost a casual shift in posture, but Reginald saw it for what it was: movement into defense, into closing off discussion. Reginald had pegged Lafontaine as highly intelligent and probably arrogant — the former attribute probably magnified by forty years of unknown human advancement. A personality like that wouldn't stand for much jostling.

"You know, *Mr. President,*" said Lafontaine, using Timken's title sarcastically, "you haven't come in here like a man who wants his farms or his sun blocker back — or, for that matter, like a man who doesn't want a pathogen released into his cities."

Reginald was about to react — to step in if possible — when the sounds of gunshots came from outside. Reginald recognized them as the weapons held by the vampire soldiers; his finely tuned ears could easily tell the report of lead rounds from those of anti-vampire rounds.

Lafontaine's head perked up. Apparently he could tell them apart, too.

Reginald snapped his head toward Timken. *"What did you do?"* he hissed.

The answer came in the form of two black shapes that exploded through the building's windows. A moment later, a pair of CPS Special Forces soldiers (not the men from the SWAT truck; these soldiers hadn't been on Reginald's roster) had grabbed Lafontaine by the arms. Reginald could feel the two vampires' bloodlust. If they'd had their helmets off, he'd see their exposed fangs.

The soldiers threw Lafontaine onto the card table, slamming him hard enough to buckle the table's legs. Then Timken was above him, and Reginald saw his Hyde face emerge — the face he kept hidden from the public behind his careful Dr. Jekyll.

With his back flat on the table and his arms held fast by the two soldiers, Lafontaine laughed.

Timken's face, very close to the human's, was red and furious. His fangs were out, glistening with saliva. His features twisted, turning his usual handsome face horrible. With a growl, he reached down and ripped Lafontaine's glasses from his face — and found himself staring into two empty eye sockets.

"In the land of the blind, the man beyond influence is king," Lafontaine laughed as Timken gaped into the two unglamourable holes.

Timken punched him hard in the face.

Reginald was shocked. In the photo he'd seen of Lafontaine, he'd had eyes. The photo had only been a few years ago. Had he taken out of his own eyes? And without those eyes, how had he navigated the room? Why, when they'd been speaking earlier, had he ticked his head between them as if meeting their eyes?

"How did you coordinate it? How are you doing this?" Timken bellowed, spraying Lafontaine with spit. Timken's bearing was terrible. An angry vampire could sometimes transcend humanity, becoming more than just a thing with fangs. What was facing Lafontaine now was more monster than man. And still the black man laughed.

Lafontaine arched as best he could with the soldiers still holding his forearms. Then he trained his empty sockets on Timken and said, "You think *I'm* blind? Look into a mirror with your beautiful vampire eyes some time. All that vision… yet throughout all these years, *you didn't see shit.*"

"If you don't start talking, I'm going to rip you apart piece by piece," Timken growled.

Lafontaine didn't answer. Instead, he looked up at the two soldiers holding him, his empty eyes boring into their black visors. The soldiers were squirming, their grip on him suddenly uncertain.

He said, "Hot in here, isn't it?"

One of the soldiers — and then, quickly afterward, the other — yelled and yanked their hands away from Lafontaine's skin. The human sat up on his elbows, smiling. The soldiers looked at their palms as if they'd never seen them before. Both of the vampire soldiers were white

— but their palms, after touching Walter Lafontaine, had turned jet black.

Lafontaine's dead eyes turned to Reginald and Timken.

"Thank you for validating my opinion of you," he said. "I expected shit... and I *got* shit." Then he turned toward the soldiers, whose gape-mouthed expressions were apparent even through their visors. "And you two," he added. "You have an hour. Better make the most of it."

He surged up from the table, snarling and swiping his hands toward Timken's face. Timken flinched back, dodging contact with the man's poisoned skin. Then Lafontaine came for Reginald with his palms out. Reginald kicked at him, caught Lafontaine in the shin. The big man staggered back and struck the table, then lunged again. Reginald dodged. He was faster than the human, but not by much. And despite Lafontaine's husky build, he seemed to have adrenaline on his side.

Lafontaine crouched. Reginald readied himself to dodge again, but instead he fell back as a great tumult of exploding glass and metal siding heralded the arrival of the vampire troops. The warehouse became a blur. As Reginald stumbled back out of the room's middle, he caught sight of the two soldiers, now writhing on the ground and screaming in agony, most of their bare arms already turning black. The newly arrived soldiers scampered away from the two infected men, climbing into the rafters, walking along the ceilings.

The humans soldiers streamed in behind the vampires. There were dozens upon dozens of them, and all were dressed in armor like the AVT used to wear, but shinier and more mobile — and, Reginald thought, with no visible weak spots. The humans didn't hesitate as the vampires had; they opened fire, striking empty air as the vampires dodged. The humans' gunfire continued, striking nothing. The vampires were too fast. But then, after a minute's worth of misses, a few bullets began to score hits. Reginald watched it happen, seeing something that stopped his undead heart: the bullets weren't flying straight. They were acting like lightning-fast heat-seeking missiles, curving in the air. With each volley of shots, the bullets came nearer and nearer their targets.

Timken had taken shelter beside Reginald. And now, seeming alien, Reginald found that he could feel the president's fear after all.

"Those weapons," Reginald told him. "They're *learning.*"

The bullets arced more and more accurately with each burst. And as he watched it happen, Reginald noticed a second thing: the troops were holding their weapons, but the rifles were also attached to the soldiers' waists by what looked like hinged robotic arms. He could hear motors in the arms whirr as the soldiers moved and fired. The bullets were learning to seek their cool targets, and the weapons' sights were learning the vampires' movement patterns. They were outmatched. Desperately. It was only a matter of time before they would all be dying on the ground, infected with the black plague.

More bursts of fire, now carefully controlled. The humans had settled into a diamond-shaped pattern around Lafontaine, who was casually wiping his arms and neck with a handkerchief as vampires began to burst into sparks around him. They dropped like insects knocked out of the air, striking the building's floor, clutching themselves and screaming. The formation of humans moved into an orderly, unrushed procession across the floor, with Lafontaine in the middle.

The second wave of vampire soldiers arrived, heavily

armored as a failsafe measure and intended for deployment only in the case of something catastrophic. The humans' bullets plinked off the new vampires' armor. They marched forward, feeling cocksure, their weapons raised. The lead-shooters, stocked with armor-piercing rounds, coughed fire, and humans began to fall. The tables slowly swung; several humans struck the floor. Others dove for cover, scrambling breathlessly away.

One of the humans threw a round device into the middle of the warehouse. Reginald knew it wasn't a normal grenade and turned away, but the throw had gone to the other side of the room. It detonated in an explosion of brilliant light, and when Reginald took his arm from his eyes, it came away sunburnt. He watched it heal, now pushing Timken backward. He had no love for the president, but right now it was us versus them, and "us" meant vampires.

More vampire troops arrived, all heavily armored. The humans seemed to have exhausted their reserves; anyone who would ever join this firefight was already here. Fewer vampires fell. More humans threw ultraviolet grenades, but they didn't have enough to make a dent. They'd struck hard and fast, and they'd taken the vampires by surprise, but the humans reached their limit as the battle wore on. There simply weren't enough of them. Thanks to the redundant ring of troops, it looked like the vampires might triumph after all, but Reginald couldn't help but wonder about the eighteen places where the humans still had them held tight... and what would happen afterward, when the human leader lay dead.

Lafontaine, watching the firefight around him, looked unconcerned. He looked directly at Reginald and gave him a little wave just as an enormous bus-style recreational vehicle crashed through the building's far wall, its windows and tires armored. The thing barreled directly at Reginald and Timken, forcing them to dive aside. Then men dove out of the bus, streaming from its doors and top hatch, and as something happened at Reginald's back, he turned to see two of the newly arrived humans wrapping the president's neck with silver and begin dragging him away.

The human formation collapsed back into the RV in such an orderly way, it had to have been rehearsed. Less than ten seconds later, most of the humans were inside — save Lafontaine, the two men holding him, and three remaining gunmen fanned out as cover. Then Lafontaine walked up to Timken, who was weakened by the silver, and slapped him on the back.

"Come on in!" he yelled.

Lafontaine laughed, then climbed the RV's steps. The two humans dragged Timken up behind him, the remaining gunmen followed, and then the big bus's door closed.

The vampire troops, undeterred, stormed the door. They scratched. They ripped aluminum from the frame. One of them reached inside, past the RV's outer shell, and was blown explosively backward. He shook his head, confused, and stormed forward. Others reached in, were similarly repelled, then fell to the dusty floor. They recovered, regrouped, and charged again, only to be repelled and knocked onto their backs. And the humans inside the bus, watching the trampoline-like display, began to laugh.

"Goddammit, you assholes!" Reginald bellowed at the soldiers. "That's a mobile *home!* You can't go in unless he invites you!"

Then Lafontaine, holding one end of Timken's silver leash, waved through the window as the RV backed out and drove away.

NINE

Escape To New York

They tried to pursue, but there was no point. The RV was unassailable. No vampire could enter without an invite, and it couldn't be slowed down without artillery owing to its armored wheels. A few of the more headstrong soldiers tried to follow anyway, but the humans, emerging from the RV's top hatch, easily picked them off. Soon the humans' mobile home was just dust on the moon-lit horizon, and the president was gone.

But that wasn't all Lafontaine had in store. He'd expected treachery from the vampires and had gotten their duplicitous best... and that was apparently enough justification to send the cavalry after the remainders, to finish the job.

As the surviving troops (plus the dying ones; it seemed cruel to leave them) were loading up to leave, a row of human vehicles summited the rise and began screaming toward the warehouse. They were shooting the minute they cleared the horizon, and they were carrying weapons much larger than those the human troops had just displayed. Something like a rocket struck the Town Car

Reginald had arrived in just as the driver was reaching for the door handle, and Reginald, who was behind the SWAT truck with Brian, leapt back as the car erupted in flame. But the explosion wasn't the worst of it; the driver emerged from the blast intact but speckled with black spots as if he'd been hit by a balloon filled with ink. So Lafontaine hadn't been bluffing; the bio weapon could indeed be put into ordnance. A relatively safe form of ordnance for those using it, as it turned out — seeing as the weapon didn't appear to harm humans.

The human trucks rolled on, firing their guns, re-aiming their rockets as the Town Car burned.

Reginald shoved Brian into the SWAT truck, then shouted for the remaining troops to haul ass. They were inside and had the rear doors closed in an instant, just as a second blast rocked the vehicle on its tires. Reginald stumbled past the jumbled and shell-shocked soldiers, yelling at the driver to *MOVE*, but a UV grenade flew through the still-ajar front door like a molotov cocktail and they all turned away, hunched in duck-and-covers. The blast incinerated the driver and severed Brian's left arm, but Brian shouted that as long as he had one arm and one leg, he was getting them the fuck out. He dove into the driver's seat atop the ash, slammed his foot onto the gas, and took off along the bumpy road, his arm slowly regrowing as the truck bounced sickeningly with gunshots and impact.

As they drove, two other SWAT trucks joined them like a caravan: the extra troops Timken had sent in order to ignore his strategist and get them all killed. The humans turned to pursue the three vehicles while the vampire trucks fought for roadspace, firing at their rear. Brian jostled for position, his shameless self-preservation quickly moving them to the front of the line — something Brian would be able to justify later because he didn't want either

100

side to win. Then another of the huge shells struck the truck at the rear, but the new shell must not have been laced with poison because Reginald, looking through the cracked rear windows, watched as black-clad vampires boiled out and leapt onto two of the human vehicles. As the trucks churned dust on the road, the crawling vampires punched through the human vehicles' plated sides, crawled in, and painted the insides with the occupants' blood.

Only one human vehicle remained, but it was bigger than the rest. It surged forward, then turned on a set of enormous ultraviolet lights mounted to its top. The driver of the rear vehicle caught fire and the truck careened side-ways, crashing into a ditch. The soldiers in Reginald's vehicle ducked down, but the light was intense enough that Reginald still caught a reflected burn, winced, and had to crawl into a corner to heal. While he crouched and waited for his skin to repair, he looked around the truck's interior, exchanging looks with the other vampires. As he locked eyes with them — with the big, strong, balls-out soldiers who'd tried to take what wasn't theirs and had gotten burned — he realized that they were all terrified. Their looks and their fear made him furious. *They* were the ones who'd started this. *They* were the species who'd struck first in the war, who'd driven the humans to fight back. *They* were the ones who'd betrayed the plan they'd asked Reginald to form — the plan they'd threatened him all the way to New York in order to get. And now *they* wanted to cower and stare at him with desperate, panicked looks as if he were their mommy? It made him want to grab them by the necks and rip out their voice boxes — and right now, they might even be weak enough for him to do it.

"GET THE FUCK UP!" he yelled as the truck bounced over the rutted, seldom-used road. The SWAT vehicle was jostling like a contained earthquake. Bodies were being

tossed from side to side; things were falling on Reginald's head; the ride was unseating his feet as he stood to watch the rear door. The inside of the truck was covered with blood, and so was Reginald's shirt. But still the fighting men who'd begun this stayed down, hiding.

Something inside Reginald snapped. In their weak-willed state, he could make the men at his feet do whatever he wanted — mass-glamour them into fighting, make them jump out and clog the road with their bodies. But he was too furious. He kicked at one man along the wall, but the soldier just cowered, his world shaken. Humans had always been like sheep. Now they were biting back, and nobody knew how to handle it.

Reginald looked around at the weapons inside the vehicle, stocked hurriedly from the hodge-podge vampire arsenal, then grabbed a belt studded with grenades. He had no idea if they were new grenades or old duds that might blow his hand off, but he didn't care. He was a vampire. He could take pain. And if his head was severed and he died? Well, then at least it would all be over.

He held up the belt, then pulled every pin. By the time he'd pulled the last, moving as fast as his non-fast body would allow, the first grenade had been armed for long enough to blow. He slammed the rear door open, then tossed the belt out. The first grenade blew before it hit the ground, and the others followed like Chinese firecrackers. Reginald felt shrapnel kiss the flesh of his arm and stomach, then clenched through the pain and watched as the explosion slipped under the tires of the human vehicle, blowing a hole through the floor bright enough to leave an afterimage on Reginald's retinas. The truck leapt into the air and then canted dead onto its side. And then they were ahead — and the road, to the front and behind, was clear.

As the air fell quiet, with only the purr of the engine

violating the solace of the night, Reginald looked anew at the vampire soldiers on the floor of the SWAT truck. He suddenly realized what he was looking at. These men weren't real vampires. Of course they weren't; they'd been turned after the war. They'd never really had to fight, had never really been tested. They were too green for the conflict they were facing. They were boys for whom vampirism meant the ability to lift heavy things, nothing more. They'd trained as soldiers because it was a job as good as any other, but they'd never expected to face an adversary.

During the drive back to the city, it became apparent that Lafontaine had sent out word that the vampires were not to be trusted, and that the rebellion had begun. Pockets of humans had emerged from nowhere — armed and lining the major roads like groups of highwaymen, ready with liquid booby traps. They'd blocked the roads with old vehicles. They'd laid spikes on the road. They were a mix of humans in normal clothing and those in armor, all of them equally deadly.

Brian stopped the SWAT truck in an open stretch, then turned to Reginald. The others looked up at him with puppy dog eyes. With his irritation mostly in-hand, Reginald took control, knowing that anything less would leave them all dead. He elected for a pulse reconnaissance strategy: a vampire scout would run forward and report back, and only *then* would the truck proceed. The humans, luckily, didn't seem to be looking for them in particular, and didn't appear to be arranged in such a way as to prevent them, specifically, from traveling back to USVC, which was the only place Reginald could think to go, seeing as Nikki had stayed behind. So they were able to eke around the highwayman groups for a long time, and when they finally got the report that there was an impassable barrier in the road, they left the truck and continued on foot.

They passed the barrier by staying away from the road and well in the weeds, eyeing the obstruction with interest. The roadblock was staffed by at least two dozen humans with guns. Brian wanted to use Reginald's time-pausing ability to blitz through the humans and kill them all before they knew what was coming, but Reginald argued that their best chance of making it back to the city center relied on not leaving a trail of death behind them. So they dodged and evaded, staying in the deep shadows, running when they could with Brian carrying Reginald in his arms like a gigantic baby. And by the time they made it to the Hudson River, Reginald had one very distinct thought: if the human gangs they'd seen in the wildlands outside of New York were any indication, there were far more humans left in the world than the five million predicted by the census. And all of them, it seemed, were ready to fight.

Reginald wondered if he was locking himself in a prison when they reached the bridge, when they crossed into Manhattan, when they navigated the used-to-be-protected vampire streets and found the rest of the supposedly-sparse city alive with human activity and the scent of human blood. While his spine prickled with fear and prophecy, he couldn't help but be aroused by all of the humanity he sensed around him. He'd never been a hunter and he'd never been a killer, but there were so *many* of them. So many of them after so long without them... and their smell, here and now, was so incredibly intoxicating. How had they hidden that smell for all this time? How had the vampires never known?

They entered the building using the access code that Brian had been given, then made their way from the loading dock into the elevators and up to the higher floors.

Reginald didn't want to talk to anyone. He didn't want to hear from Claude or Charles or Walker, and he didn't want to find a way to rescue Timken. He just wanted to go to his room. He wanted to sleep, or take a bath, or possibly enter a fugue and talk to Maurice. The sun was finally rising, and the humans were laying claim to their half of the day. And, he thought wryly, just look at all they'd been able to handle during the nighttime, while the vampires were supposed to reign.

Nikki met him at the door, her eyes red, then wrapped him in a hug and refused to let him go. They collapsed onto the bed together, Reginald exhausted from exertion and Nikki exhausted from emotion. Uneasy sleep followed. Reginald didn't enter the codex or his bloodline, but his dreams were haunted by the souls of vampires — *souls* as his higher mind imagined them, burning in fires and dying screaming. He dreamed that Maurice was there with him as he watched it all happen, and then in the way that dreams are, the two of them were suddenly and inexplicably playing cards in a place where it was dark, sitting on rock, a folding metal chair in the background with a silver chain draped over its back. Maurice laid down all of his cards, then said, *Gin*. Reginald looked up into Maurice's face and said, *I thought we were playing poker* and Maurice replied, *That's your problem*. Then Reginald woke up, covered in a sheen of sweat.

He'd slept the entire day. Nikki had slept less, and when he opened his sluggish eyes and saw her, she was across the room, sitting on a padded chair in front of the vanity mirror wearing only a bra and panties, brushing her long, dark hair. She looked haggard despite also looking beautiful; beautiful was on the outside while haggard was in the depths of her eyes when she looked over, seeing he'd woken.

"Tell me I'm back in Columbus," he said. "There never was a human rebellion. There never was even a war. We're human. Later we're going to get dressed and go to work, and Maurice will be there. After work, we'll visit our ten-year-old friend Claire. I will be tormented by Todd Walker, who will put a Whoopie Cushion on my seat."

"Maybe just the last," said Nikki, smiling.

Reginald rolled onto his back and studied the popcorn ceiling. A long, long, *long* time ago, he used to watch reality TV shows where people bought houses, fixed them up, and sold them for a profit. They always hated popcorn ceilings. Why? This one wasn't so bad.

"Have you checked the news?" he asked. "Or Fangbook?"

Nikki gave him a look that was kind, and almost protective. He tried hard to keep his mind out of hers, but her look said everything he couldn't read from her mind or her blood: that it was a question he didn't want to know the answer to.

"Just tell me."

"They were all just waiting," she said, and Reginald found he didn't need her to clarify who "they" were. "What you told me you saw on your way back is happening everywhere. Fangbook is just sad. Remember how you used to wish Fangbook would just go away, because it was a haven for bloodlust and the glorification of murder?"

He nodded.

"Well, now it's like a support group. At best, it's like Facebook used to be. You remember how Facebook was?"

"I was never really into Facebook. It was a haven for douchebaggery and the glorification of stupid internet memes."

"Fangbook is now just vampires screaming and cowering, as told by status updates and photos. I scrolled back in my feed when I saw what was populating because I was curious. Usually Fangbook is quiet during the day, but today it was more awake than ever. You read through it for long enough, and it starts to sound like *Night of the Living Dead* in reverse. All the monsters hiding in basements, peeking out to see gangs of non-stumbling, non-infected, non-dead human beings walking through their yards with stakes and silver and guns and torches."

"They're in the cities?" said Reginald.

"No, mostly just in the wildlands, where the hippies live outside of the government's 'tyranny.' But if you ask me — which you shouldn't because my husband is the genius logician who knows literally everything — it seems like they're not even trying to get into the cities. It's like they're just trying to move their pieces into position at this point, before they strike. Like in chess."

"Why is this entire thing one big chess metaphor?" said Reginald. "I'm tired of chess."

"But you're so good at chess," she said.

And he was. So in the hour before sunset, as they sat safe (for now) in the well-guarded USVC building, Reginald tried to align his own pieces. He sped through web pages as quickly as he could click and scroll, trying to absorb information into his mind like... well, like Claire could. And with that thought, his head perked up. At first he felt inspired. But another, much more sinister emotion came on its heels.

"Claire," he said.

Nikki had dressed and was pacing the room, fidgeting with her earrings. Nikki had never been big on jewelry, but when her sister had died, she'd made a trek into the wildlands community where Jackie had lived and died a natural but somewhat early death and picked up a load of Jackie's belongings. One of the things Jackie had saved and protected throughout all of her tumultuous years was their mother's gold. What little jewelry Nikki had had when Reginald had met her had been silver; she'd never liked the look of gold. But her turn to vampire had changed that, out of necessity.

Right now was the least logical time to fuss with jewelry, especially for Nikki. But she was doing it so she'd have something to do — so she wouldn't just have to sit and wait and pray to a God she never really believed in, and that she wasn't sure would want her now anyway.

She stopped pacing. "What about Claire?"

Reginald had been talking to himself. Now he looked up and answered her anyway.

"She's in a vampire city."

"She'll be okay."

"That's not a given," he said.

She walked over, then stooped and wrapped her arms around Reginald's torso. "No, Reginald. She'll be fine. When you came back this morning, after I woke up, Brian came in and showed me his cell phone. It had been lying on his nightstand, and it was full of text messages. Non-network text messages. I'm no genius, but if you were to look at the network they came from, I'd guess it'd say something like 'The Lollipop Network,' or whatever else Claire had thought was amusing at the time."

Reginald felt himself relax. All Nikki had told him was that Claire had sent Brian some messages — meshing her mind with electrons as usual, pushing messages directly from her brain to the closest mobile device to her friends, or so she'd thought — but Reginald could feel pacification rolling over him like a comfortable blanket. The feeling wasn't coming from facts; it was coming from Nikki. It felt like she was casting a calming spell on him without even meaning to do so. Or maybe she *did* mean to do so. Maybe their blood bond had simply made a quiet activity between a couple feel more real.

"The first few messages were warnings," she said. "Disturbingly *specific* warnings about Walter Lafontaine — which is a name that, as far as I've seen, isn't known by the general population. She knew you were going to meet with him, and she warned you not to. She warned us that it was a trap. If only we'd seen that phone, Reginald."

It didn't matter. They'd made it back alive. All they'd lost was the architect of the world's murder.

"You can't take a cell phone on a raid," he told her.

"It wasn't supposed to be a raid. It was supposed to be a negotiation."

"Well," he said, gesturing vaguely, "I guess that shows what we know. Me being a genius vampire mastermind and all."

"Don't do that."

Normally he'd wave her away when she told him not to deprecate himself, but this time her words felt particularly poignant, and he let them settle. He wasn't the same man he'd been. He wasn't the same vampire he'd been. He didn't look any different, but he was a little stronger. A little faster. He didn't eat junk food. He drank a healthy amount of blood. He ran and he trained despite the fact that it couldn't help him, just to prove to himself that he could. And he didn't wallow in self-pity. Self-pity did nothing. It was the purest form of self-indulgence: self-important egoism disguised as penance. But self-pity had never helped anyone, ever, and he knew it.

"The later texts read like a live recap of your journey back, also oddly specific. She was able to tell where you were and how you were doing, right up until you got back here. Honestly, I wish I'd known so that I could follow along. I was worried sick. As usual, I have no idea how she did any of it."

"She probably plugged into the satellites. Or extrapolated what had to happen next from the information she already had, assuming she had the visibility she can't always count on having. Or maybe she extrapolated from the things that she *could* see easily, or glean from news reports. Or all of the above."

Nikki shrugged. It hadn't been a real question.

Reginald sighed. Maybe she would be fine. In a literal sense, Claire knew almost everything, assuming she could access the information. She was the closest thing to omniscient that the mortal plane had ever known. He imagined her dodging threats as she saw them coming, always staying one step ahead — not unlike what Reginald could do with his hyper-awareness, when he stopped time and analyzed his choices. He imagined Claire doing much the same, and felt better.

"I guess she'll be okay," he said. But that was only half of his Claire thoughts. Half of the reason his head had popped up and he'd said her name.

"I want to call her," said Reginald. "I need her mind. I need her to help me analyze the human activity."

"You can't call her," said Nikki.

Reginald ignored her, picking up his cell phone. Claire didn't have a cell phone because she didn't need one, but the house she lived in had a phone, and she'd had it activated. There was Skype. There was even email. He began to dial.

"I said, you can't call her," said Nikki.

"Why not?"

"She left. She's not at home."

Reginald's sense of temporary peace broke like a dropped plate. "Oh."

But as his head was sagging, he heard a knock on the door. He looked up. Nikki started to rise, but she didn't make it past a partial crouch. The door had an electronic swipe lock. It clicked, and the door opened. And there in the doorway was a young woman with long, light brown hair, dressed in jeans and a red top.

"Hey," said Claire.

TEN

Meet The New Boss, Same As The Old Boss

Reginald was furious with Claire for crossing the country on her own, but Claire waved him off as usual, assuring him that it was fine. She'd sneaked out of her house in full light, making her way across the city and darting through the gate. Once outside, she'd been safe. She was walking in the sun, probably developing a sunburn owing to her pale skin and lack of regular sun exposure, so no human would think she was a vampire unless they scoped her and found her cold — and even if they *did* scope her, they wouldn't know *what* to think. She'd then stolen a car and made her way to a converted hospital on the periphery of the wildlands that she'd seen helicopters fly out of in the past, presumably to scope the wildlands for the Vampire Nation. She'd found the helicopter fueled, had climbed inside, and had flown it.

When Nikki, aghast, asked how the hell she'd flown a helicopter, Claire just waved her hands mysteriously in the air. The television came on, then turned off. Brian's cell phone, in the other room, rang. The lights turned on and off, and the electronic door clicked open and closed. The air conditioning came on and off, and in front of them both, Claire's palms glowed with a strange blue light. Then everything stopped and she lowered her palms, and she answered Nikki's question: "I just *flew it*, and now it's on the roof." Then she pointed up, a small, innocent smile on her wide, pretty lips.

Reginald yelled at her. He said that she could easily have been killed — not just by vampires looking for humans, but also by humans looking for vampires. Claire was neither. The vampire community she'd lived in knew her as vampire, but when she used to go into the wildlands to visit her dying mother, the few vampire-friendly humans they knew had treated her as human. She didn't have fangs and she couldn't move like a vampire (or could she? Reginald suspected she might be sandbagging; getting out of the city walls wasn't simple, and Claire had glossed over it as if it were), but she was cold under their sensors. She could walk in the sun. And she could manipulate energy — an ability that Reginald, to this day, believed she'd only scratched the surface of. But as Reginald watched Claire come into his room at USVC and sit on the bed beside Nikki, all he could see in his mind were all of the dangers she had faced. And it made him angry.

Claire's response was simple and direct. "I'm 51," she said. "Get off my back, mom."

It was true. Claire hadn't had a mother in any real sense until she'd been old enough for a mother's influence to barely matter. Between the addling inflicted by Altus the incubus and the damage the vampire agent had done to her following her attack, Claire's mother hadn't returned to normal until Claire's aging had slowed, until after the writing was already on the wall. Reginald and Nikki had made decent surrogate parents ("decent" other than repeatedly leading her into apocalyptic peril), but they weren't her blood, and their influence and authority over her could only stretch so far.

Once Reginald accepted that Claire had, in fact, taken her ill-advised trip whether he liked it or not (and once he realized that all of his fears for her would go away now that she was with them), he settled down and began pumping her for information. She was only moderately helpful, but she nudged his piece further ahead on the game board than it had been before. Claire's omniscience was almost subconscious. She got impulses of foreknowl-edge in the way some people reacted to new events based on incidents in their past, and when she'd begun to fear for Reginald, Nikki, and Brian, a sort of window had opened into her archive and she'd seen it all unfold, watching the information as it funneled to her through the internet's wires and across the air. Her mind had collated and delivered that information right then, when she was in need, quite clearly. But in the absence of a traumatic event to re-open that window, Claire could only speak vaguely about the world of facts around her: *Yes*, human clusters were appearing worldwide, strategically placed as if by a master plan laid out years ago. *Yes*, there were many more humans than vampires had thought. And *yes*, all those humans out there had been playing dumb while their innovation and technology had, in fact, been growing by leaps and bounds. But beyond those vagaries, Claire had nothing. Nikki suggested glamouring her as Reginald had done before, but Reginald didn't want to do it. Glamouring a vampire always felt invasive — and Claire, he said, felt more and more like a vampire with every passing day. Nikki pushed harder, and Claire said that it was okay, that she'd do it. But still Reginald hedged, and finally the debate was short-circuited when Ophelia knocked on the door and told them that the president needed to see them. She didn't make it sound like a request.

Reginald's deeper mind caught what Ophelia had said right away, but it took his top level of consciousness a moment to catch up. They were walking back toward the elevator by the time her words hit home.

"You got Timken back?"

She shook her head. "President *Toussant*."

Reginald realized now why Ophelia hadn't summoned Brian too, and hence why Brian had been available to keep an eye on Claire while Nikki and Reginald went with the general. Brian could never, ever be in the same room with Claude again. He'd rip the man apart. Forty years wasn't enough time to heal the grudge Brian would never forget: Claude had killed his maker, and Brian was big and strong and fast enough to do something about it.

"Timken is dead?" Reginald said, feeling like he'd missed several memos.

"It's de facto," said Ophelia. "Mr. Toussant was the vice president, so he's president in the actual president's absence."

"So you're just *acting* as if he's dead," said Reginald. He turned to Nikki. "Like when they hire someone to replace you when you go on maternity leave."

The move was puzzling without being puzzling at all. Claude could lead the Vampire Nation just fine while remaining vice president. There was no reason to claim the presidency, seeing as he'd just have to give it back the minute Timken was returned. But on the other hand, it made sense because Claude was, in Reginald's words, "a gigantic cocksucker." Reginald filed the information for later consideration.

They made their way back to the meeting room, meeting up with Charles at the door. When they walked in,

Reginald found the mood and the tableau identical, only with Claude now in Timken's chair. He suddenly felt like he was in a daytime soap opera that had found itself short an actor: *This week, the role of Nicolas Timken will be played by Claude Toussant.*

The minute Reginald saw Claude — the big man in his too-small suit, a black goatee on his chin, a vacant and vaguely condescending expression on his face — he charged. He shoved Ophelia aside, vaulted the table with shocking agility (his balance and coordination had improved greatly; he could have beat human gymnasts in the Olympics if he were able to touch his toes), and had his hands around the vice president's / president's throat before anyone could react. He squeezed with everything he had. His fangs came out. His blood boiled.

Claude smiled up at him. Behind him, Ophelia righted herself and sat in one of the chairs across the table from Claude — and, apparently, Reginald — as if nothing were amiss. Charles sat beside her. Then Nikki walked up to Reginald and patted him kindly on the shoulder.

"You motherfucker!" Reginald hissed. "I'm going to tear you apart!"

Claude twitched his head. Claude was too fast for Reginald to see entirety of the movement, but he did feel a very sharp pain as Claude's forehead rammed into his. He felt his scalp split, felt something liquid run across his nose and cheek. Reginald's hands let go of Claude's throat and he tumbled from the table and to the floor at Claude's feet.

Nikki pulled out a chair, then bent down to beckon Reginald from under the table. Above him, Claude gestured toward the chair.

"Give me one fucking reason I should sit in the same room with you," said Reginald, standing and wiping the blood from his forehead.

"I'm wearing fantastic cologne," said Claude.

Reginald's fangs were still out. He looked at Claude's neck and found himself longing to separate it from his body. Even if he could forgive Claude for killing Maurice (which he couldn't), the score was too thick to settle. The entire world had a score to settle with Claude Toussant. He'd been behind the murderous V-Crews, behind the war crimes, behind the rumors of death camps. Every vampire had blood on their hands, but Claude's hands were wrist-deep in an ocean of it.

"Sit down, Reginald," said Charles, settling in. He straightened first his lapels and then his hair, and Reginald marveled that throughout everything, the one thing that had never faltered was Charles's wardrobe.

Reginald looked from Charles to Claude. He couldn't fight them, and it would be pointless to try. And now that he thought about it, giving Ophelia or the others any reason to evict them from USVC was an incredibly stupid idea. First of all, logically, it was in the world's best interest to solve the situation with Lafontaine and Timken. And second, he wasn't at all sure that anyone other than he, Nikki, and Brian knew that Claire was here. She'd landed a helicopter on the roof, but the highest floors were unused, and if he knew Claire's ability, she'd probably scrambled all electronic records of her arrival without even intending to. But if the others found out, it would be one more pinch point. She wasn't a vampire, and Reginald cared about her. Just one more way for the others to gain leverage, and to put Claire right back in danger she'd so recently escaped.

With effort, Reginald sat. But before he did, he wheeled Nikki's chair across from Claude and situated himself one chair removed, so that they didn't have to sit directly across from one another. It was a ridiculous and petty move, but right now, Reginald was willing to take any tiny victories he could manage.

He looked up, and realized that everyone was looking at him.

"What?" he said.

"Well, what do we do?" Claude asked.

Reginald looked at Ophelia. "You're the general. Where's your slide show and speech filled with dehumanizing terms?"

"We're blind," said Ophelia, shaking her head. "You know as much as we know. Even our satellites are starting to blink out. All we know is that there are pockets of human hostility everywhere. The incidents we had a handle on earlier have totally degenerated because troops had to retreat when they were approached from behind."

Reginald saw something in Ophelia's eyes. He met them, challenging her.

"Or when, in a few cases, those troops were assaulted and killed," she admitted.

"So you got pantsed," said Reginald. "They walked up behind you — all of you — and just yanked. They had us pegged all along. They were just waiting."

After a moment, Ophelia said, "It seems that way."

"Did you get an idea of how many of them there were? Do you have any data at all?"

Ophelia popped up the same screen she'd used before, dimmed the lights, and projected a satellite map of New York onto the front wall. "All we really have is this," she said.

Reginald leaned forward. The map showed heat signatures, with notes and tags overlaying the projection. There were large red and orange clusters across Manhattan and the boroughs. Outside the city, beyond the bridges and tunnels, were smaller, more isolated clusters.

"Jesus," said Nikki.

"There's at least a quarter million on that map alone," said Reginald. He looked closer. The entire "abandoned" section of the city was lit up to some degree, but amongst the chaos, Reginald could see a pattern. They were mostly around the bridges and tunnels, clustered on both sides of each. At the main corridor — the blocked-off roads they'd used to enter the city's core — the red heat signatures were positioned along its entire length. It was an excellent deployment map. If Reginald were in charge of the human army, he'd have done the same: notice the single logical choke point, then mine it.

"We estimate three hundred thousand," said Ophelia. "We have similar reports from Geneva, but no visuals. Obviously it's worst around the capitols. The outlying areas won't be anywhere near this congested."

"So you assume," said Reginald.

"Well, yes."

He looked at the map again. It was bright enough to be a lit Christmas tree. "How didn't you see all these heat signatures before now?"

"We're working on the theory that they were in the tunnels," she said.

"Don't you patrol the tunnels?"

"Some. In fact, some of them are the CPC's main arteries. We actually *use* the tunnels. They're also mined, in areas where a collapse wouldn't weaken parts of the city we need for our infrastructure. But there are a lot of tunnels under New York. It's not just subways. There's sewers, utility corridors…"

"You knew this, but you didn't patrol them all?"

"We did what we could. We can only stretch so thin. There are a lot of tunnels here, and a lot of tunnels and hidey-holes in the rest of the world. We only have so many troops."

"In other words," said Nikki, "you thought you could step in and occupy enemy territory with your small peace-keeping army." She turned to Reginald. "Because that strategy has a history of working well in warfare."

"We didn't have a choice," said Claude.

Reginald stabbed an angry finger at Claude. "See, that's where you're just a big fucking fucker," he said. "That's all you've been saying from the beginning. You, Timken, Charles, even Logan. But you don't even hear yourselves. It's like you're stuck in a loop, like your brains died when your body died. I've got a theory. Do you want to hear it?"

"No," said Claude.

"I think that the mind isn't like the body. I think it can't be idle and unchanging. I think that a mind either grows or atrophies, so if you think you can just have an 'unchang-ing' mind for millennia while your body stops aging, you're deluding yourself. In the case of the mind, I think that standing still *is* decay."

Charles rolled his eyes.

"You caused this, you know," said Reginald, turning his anger on Charles. "It's right here, in the vampire codex." He tapped his head. "Humanity didn't have the edge it needed to fight you back when there were only seventy thousand vampires and seven billion humans. They had the numbers, but they were soft and complacent. They'd stopped evolving. They let everything else do their thinking for them. But you had to push them, didn't you? Your little apocalypse forced them to adapt or die. And guess what? They adapted. And now, *you're* going to die."

The conference room door opened. Reginald's head turned to see the oiled hair and bright white tombstone teeth of Todd Walker enter the room. This time, Nikki flinched to rise, but Reginald put a hand on her knee to hold her down. It was the first time either of them had seen Walker in the flesh since they'd left him chained to a pipe in the old Council building in Columbus. Since then, he'd had many titles, and most had implied that he'd finally found his niche. He'd become a professional bully and asshole.

Walker straightened his suit coat, then walked to the table and made himself comfortable beside Charles, on a slight diagonal from Nikki. Unbelievably, he winked at her.

"Sorry I'm late," he said.

Claude nodded toward Charles and Walker. "These two were both in Timken's cabinet: secretaries of something or other that I don't care about and that don't matter. But now they're like my vice presidents."

"You're not the president," said Nikki.

Claude smiled, his sinister teeth emerging from behind his black goatee.

"I stand corrected," he said. "But let's just play pretend, to keep the titles simple."

"Okay," said Reginald. He pointed toward Walker. "His title is 'cunt.'"

"That's not playing pretend," said Nikki.

Walker faked a frown. "I'm hurt. All those years working together. We're friends, you and me." And as Reginald stuck his fingers into Walker's mind — he didn't care about being improper when the subject was Walker — he saw something amazing: Walker really *did* consider them to be twisted kinds of friends. Reginald decided that people like Walker probably didn't have any genuine friends, so this was the best they could do. They probably had people they made fun of who "knew it was all in good fun" instead. And hey, thumbscrews made for strange bedfellows.

Nikki started to reply, but the exchange was pointless. Reginald gave her a look and she fell silent. They were outnumbered by douchebags. There were only two sensible people and four assholes, and just like that Reginald realized that he'd landed in a triage situation. He'd never get a sensible outcome out of these four, so the best he could do would be to *get by* and *get out*. He would need to figure out the easiest, most non-offensive way to do what they required of him, do it, and find a way to escape — keeping in mind that "escape" would probably still mean a life on the run from someone. His job was to protect Nikki, Claire, and Brian. Everything else was secondary, including his own life.

Claude extended a hand toward Walker. "Todd is our blood marshal," he said. "That basically means that in addition to being my vice president — I'm sorry, I mean my 'vice vice president' — he's been in charge of monitoring the blood stock at the farms."

Reginald understood now why Walker was here. There were two primary tasks on the table, and Claude had nailed both of them. They had to appear to be doing something to improve PR (ideally something symbolic; rescuing Timken or killing Lafontaine were at the top of that list) to give the population the appearance that everything was under control, and they had to keep the vampires of the world fed. If the blood supply dried up, panic would quickly follow.

All eyes turned to Walker. He sat back.

"We've lost control of or access to seventy-five percent of the state-controlled blood farms," he said. "It looks very intentional. Before we lost imagery, we were beginning to get the distinct impression that the biggest clusters outside of New York and Geneva were around the farms."

"How the hell did they coordinate all of this?" said Charles.

Reginald looked into Charles's eyes. "Their leader removed his eyes and could see," said Reginald. "Clearly, they've figured a few things out over the past forty years."

"But how?"

Reginald could only shake his head, suddenly wishing he could put his big brain to use on the other side. He'd already formed a mental image of the human world as it had actually existed over the past decades, as opposed to the way the vampires had imagined it existing. There had to be huge underground manufacturing facilities and research labs. Wet benches and medical equipment capable of growing a biological weapon able to preferentially attack the vampire agent but not human cells. The humans, Reginald had already realized, clearly knew far more about vampires than vampires did.

"I doubt we could understand their methods without years of prerequisite background," said Reginald. "How would you explain a cell phone to a caveman?"

"Ooga," Nikki suggested.

Walker cleared his throat and resumed. "There are only a handful of farms that can still operate, produce, and ship blood without incident. We've ordered emergency protocols, and..."

"You're going to drain them dry," said Nikki, realization dawning.

"*Close* to dry," said Walker. "But we can't kill them, because then that would be it for our blood supply. Oh, there's plenty more blood out there in the wetsacks who are attacking us, but it's like fresh water in the middle of the ocean, seeing as we can't get near it. We've spent a lot of time experimenting to find the ideal drain point in situations like this, where we drain them enough to get as large of a batch as possible without impairing our ability to, in a day or two, get more."

"We've also increased CPC presence around the remaining farms," Ophelia added, bringing the room lights back up.

Walker nodded. "Now, in addition, there are the small private farms. A lot of vampires keep their own humans, and a few have a small herd and re-sell as organic or all-natural or some other horseshit. We keep records of all of them, and we're moving out now, to seize what we can, under order of national emergency."

"What about HemoByte?" said Nikki.

Walker nodded. It was the simplest of gestures, but Reginald marveled at how odd it was coming from Todd Walker. The nod had acknowledged Nikki's point, no more and no less — but it also meant that Walker was speaking to them as equals. It was strange to remember the way he'd tortured them both at the office, and that they were all sitting around a table to discuss the stealing of people's blood.

"We do have HemoByte, yes. But taking pills isn't the same as drinking, and while it will keep vampires from starving, they won't like it. It won't keep them from panicking. But we've pulled in all of the stores we can find and are already distributing rations in the city. But it's a fragile balance. The more we look like we're in emergency mode — I mean, standing in line for a ration of fucking *HemoByte* instead of going to your fridge for the real thing? — well, the more people will panic, and then it just gets worse and worse. We want to prevent riots by acting like all is well, but all *isn't* well, and we need to keep them from starving."

Reginald shook his head. He didn't want to say what

was on his mind, which was that he'd been predicting all of this for decades, and nobody had listened.

"You've apparently done a lot of thinking about this," he said instead.

Walker nodded. "We've had to. You've heard the reports that a lot of the blood stock is becoming sick? Well, we've been understating the problem a little. It was starting to reach epidemic levels before all of this happened. The need to have a Plan B has been on a lot of minds lately — mine most of all."

"What's causing it?"

"We don't know. At first we just thought it was flu. We were going to institute a vaccine program, but..." He stalled, unsure how to continue. Then Reginald realized why.

"But you couldn't synthesize the vaccine, could you?"

Walker shook his head. "I asked our eggheads. They said they couldn't. I said that was ridiculous; they were our *eggheads*. But then I realized that really, they're just cooks. They need a recipe, and in the war, the recipes for how exactly to synthesize flu vaccines were all lost. It was like a scavenger hunt. They had to look all over, and they already had a handful of vaccines — measles, chicken pox, a few of the biggies — but the flu wasn't one of them."

"The flu vaccine was a dead end anyway," said Ophelia. "It looks like flu, but it sticks around too long. Unless they're passing it back and forth. Can that happen, or does the virus eventually die off in a small population?"

Reginald put his face in his palm. "Jesus Christ, you don't even know how to diagnose it. Don't you have any doctors? People who got their training before some asshole drank their blood and killed them?"

"Of course there are doctors," Ophelia snapped. "Good ones! It's just that..."

"Maybe they'll all die," Charles interrupted. Everyone turned to look at him, and his head retreated like a turtle's.

Walker glanced at Charles, then looked back to Reginald. "To be clear," he said, "if you think I'm saying that there's a human pandemic out there and coming to save us, I'm not. As far as we can tell, the wild population doesn't even seem to be affected by whatever's hitting the stock."

"Inbreeding," said Nikki.

Reginald shook his head. "Not enough generations have passed. Besides, the captive populations are big enough that I don't think brothers are screwing their sisters quite yet." Then something occurred to Reginald and he looked at Claude, not Walker. "Why are you bringing this up?" he asked.

Claude gave a small shrug. "We were wondering if maybe we could weaponize it," he said.

"*Weaponize it?* Are you telling me that you want to use whatever's affecting the blood stock to create a plague?"

"A human plague. Sure."

This time, Reginald put his face in *both* of his palms.

"Why not?" said Claude, a pout in his voice. "They have a plague ready for us!"

Reginald looked up, using his hands to rub his cheeks, pulling them long in exasperation. He looked the new vampire president squarely in the eyes. "You," he said, "are so stupid that I literally can't believe you've survived this long."

Claude looked around at the others for help.

"First of all, I think we all know that Larry, Moe, and Curly in the vampire science labs will *never* figure out how to manipulate a virus. So it's already moot."

"We could capture human scientists and force them to do it," said Charles.

"Second," Reginald barged on, ignoring Charles, "even if you *could* create a weapon, you'd be like a kid with a stick of dynamite, just as likely to kill yourself as anything else. Third, you don't know that it wouldn't cross species and kill off something else that's vital to the ecosystem. And lastly, if you do manage to kill all of the humans, *you will have killed all of the humans.* How will you eat *then?* The worst thing you could do in a plan like that would be to succeed."

Claude ignored the insult, tapping the surface of the table with one of the pens from Timken's desk set. "What weapons do we have, then?" he asked.

Ophelia ticked off the options on her fingers. "Guns of all kinds. Artillery. A few bombs. We can get their planes flying if we need to, and we know the locations of their missile bases, where…"

Reginald shook his head, unable to believe what he was hearing. "You're going to nuke them?"

"Why not?" she said. "As long as we don't strike near a vampire population center, we're impervious to the radiation, and…"

"Jesus fucking Christ," said Reginald. "Let's try this again: if you poison the Earth and kill them off, what are we going to eat to survive?"

"They won't all die," said Walker.

"Just be horribly poisoned and mutated, I guess," said Reginald. "Hey Todd, when you were human, did you like eating rancid steak?"

"No nukes," said Claude.

"Guns, then," said Ophelia. "And of course, our hands and teeth."

"And when they shoot you with their smart bullets?" said Reginald.

"Or hit you with that poison shit that turns your skin black?" Nikki added.

"Fucking hell, they're *animals!*" Claude blurted, standing. "We're stronger than they are! Faster! Better! You're telling me we can't get near them?"

"Hey, be my guest," said Reginald. "Just don't be surprised when your dick rots off."

Claude paced, shaking his head. Fury radiated from him. "Can we wear some kind of protection?" he asked. "Something that will keep that shit off of us?"

"Sure," said Reginald. "Get a raincoat."

"Like at a Gallagher show," said Nikki.

"What's Gallagher?" said Charles.

"Not to be a downer," said Reginald, "but they've also got 'that shit' in their bullets. I saw it blow out of a rocket of some kind, too. And given that it doesn't seem to harm them, there's no reason they couldn't make bombs out of it. Drop one right on us, from a missile bunker you missed. Forget nukes; conventional explosives would be plenty to spread it far and wide. Whoever's hit dies an hour later. Maybe they even find a way to make it communicable, which so far, thankfully, it doesn't seem to be, and then once we're gone, they party on our ashes. Game over."

Claude paced. "This is intolerable."

"Payback's a bitch, huh?"

Claude shot Reginald a look that was full of venom. So Reginald, already at the edge, decided to press further. He added, "Guess you shouldn't have killed Maurice either, huh?"

"What does that have to do with anything?"

There was a cup filled with hot, blood-spiked coffee in front of Reginald. He threw it at Claude, scoring a hit.

Claude's skin turned red, then rapidly healed. Reddish-brown coffee soaked into the white shirt under his suit.

"Because your mother," Reginald answered, realizing it wasn't one of his best zingers.

They sat for a moment, everyone looking at everyone else as the truth settled in: there was very little they could do. They couldn't touch the humans and the humans could push in and touch them plenty. They might receive the emergency blood shipments that Walker said were coming and they might not. They might be able to keep the population fed for a few more weeks and they might not. It was all up to the humans. They couldn't fight back one-on-one for fear of the humans' biological weapon unless they wore biohazard suits, but something told Reginald that the humans would be prepared for that contingency. Somehow, a man without eyes had found a way to see, and somehow, an oppressed, decimated population of savages had managed to arrange their pieces across the game board in stealth, ready to pop up and strike all at once. They would have ways around something as mundane as bloodsuckers in baggies. Even suit-slitting knives would be an effective offense.

The door opened again and a vampire in uniform rushed into the room. He conversed briefly with Ophelia, and she ran off behind him. She returned five minutes later, then turned to face the others, all of whom were eagerly waiting.

"Lafontaine just called," she said.

Claude jerked his head around. "Put him on!"

"He just talked for a few minutes," said Ophelia. "He did all of the talking; I just listened. Then he hung up."

"Then get the recording. Play it back!"

Ophelia shook her head. "He called my cell phone. I left it at reception to charge."

"He called *your cell phone?*" But immediately after saying it, Claude waved his big hand to indicate that the point was moot. If Lafontaine's people could email the president, they could snoop out a general's phone number. Of course, the fact that he'd called a private number would also mean that the call couldn't easily be traced, which may well have been why he'd done it. So Claude changed his question. "Well, what did he say?" he asked.

"He wants to meet again," said Ophelia. "Tomorrow at midnight. He gave me a location, not far from the last meetup. He said that if we try to pull anything again, he'll be ready again. He said to remind you how easily they'd anticipated everything the first time — how he knew you'd try to grab him and so had covered himself with the disease, how he'd known our troops would come in armed and how they'd been prepared for it. He said..." She swallowed. "He said to be sure to tell you that he is smarter than you — and that humans, as a species, are smarter than all of us." She stopped, then swallowed again.

"Okay," said Claude, trying to appear in control. "What does he want?"

"He wants us to release the prisoners at the farms they have under siege. Every single one of them, non-negotiable. He says he'll give us Timken in return, so that we can 'save face and run off with our tails between our legs.' Then, after the stock are all safely away from the farms and under their protection, he'll pull his men out and let our guards and technicians go."

Claude shook his head. "That's 75 percent of the blood supply. We can't just give them all up. There has to be another way." He turned to Walker for confirmation.

Walker sighed. "Honestly, those farms are lost anyway," he said. "Once we solve this — *if* we solve this — we can get new stock and rebuild, but we can't do anything until

130

they release the facilities. Plus, those standoffs are using up a lot of CPC manpower. There's no way, at this point, to force a solution with that stock. They've had a taste of revolution. There will be nothing but problems if we don't find a way to start fresh, with fresh humans. Right now, giving up the stock might be doing ourselves a favor. It'll at least flush the system."

Claude took a long moment, looking around the table. "Fine," he said. "Make the arrangements."

ELEVEN

Compromise

Reginald felt deja vu.

Once again, he suited up. Claude, who was the only other person going on the mission, prepared beside him. This time, they were suiting up just enough to protect themselves but not enough to fight... which, in the end, made the deja vu that much more intense because Reginald hadn't known his companions had planned to fight the first time. So as he prepared, he wondered at the intentions of those around him. Would Claude and Ophelia try to mass troops in secret to assault the humans as they'd done last time? Or had they actually heard Lafontaine's message and accepted that whatever extra troops they tried to send, the humans would be more than prepared to meet them?

Suspicious, Reginald asked Claire to sift through the building's computer network to see if she could find any secret plans pertaining to the mission. Were there charts and troop assignments on any of the hard drives? Had there been unexpected gun or armor deployments? Were Claude and Ophelia sending communications back and forth that looked like plotting for anything beyond what Lafontaine had allowed?

But there was nothing. Claude seemed to accept that he'd been outmatched, and that the Vampire Nation's best (and possibly only) chance would be to take what they could get, fall back, and then reassess. Claude had heard what Walker said about the farms the same as Reginald had: they were already lost. Fighting for them now would be an act of ego instead of logic, and would do more harm than good.

So he suited up, donning a set of body armor as Lafontaine's directives seemed to allow, watching as Claude did the same. With only two of them going, there was no room for funny business. But he still made sure to pocket his phone, then asked Claire to watch whatever satellites were in the area and call him if she saw anything funny. He wanted to be the first to know if more vampire troops arrived, if there was any sign that Claude wasn't playing fair. And if that happened, Reginald would blow the whistle himself. Then he'd change sides if the humans would let him — or die if they wouldn't.

Nikki asked Claire what would happen on the upcoming mission, seeing as she'd intuited danger before and during the earlier mission. Claire told Nikki that she could see nothing. Reginald said that Claire's blankness proved there would be no foul play, but Nikki pointed out that Claire's predictions were far from predictable, and that hearing her prophecies was a bit like trying to tune into a distant TV station whose reception popped in and out of clarity depending on the weather.

Nikki hated that Reginald was going and that she wasn't, but Reginald told her that there was a hierarchy of importance at work here, and that as much as he loathed Claude, keeping the vampire population alive was now at the top of that hierarchy. Other than Claire (who was barely human, if at all), there were no humans left that he felt any real attachment to; everyone else he cared about had fangs and drank blood. So he had to do what he could, and right now, that meant making the exchange work. It meant walking in beside Claude, and it meant walking out with the mastermind of the global holocaust on his other side. The entire endeavor was beyond repugnant, but it was, at the moment, what needed to be done.

So Reginald would go. Claude would go. Everyone else would stay behind. Lafontaine had allowed for a party of two only, and had added that spotters would be looking out for vampire backup for miles around. If they saw any, the deal was off. He'd kill Timken; he'd kill Claude and Reginald; he'd burn the blood farms and the other points of siege.

As Reginald double-checked the straps on his vest, he looked over at Claude's large form. He met his eyes, trying to prod without prodding. Since their first encounter on the TGV, Claude had always kept a firm mental wall up around Reginald, but feeling the edges of Claude's emotions now, Reginald found nothing alarming. He looked at him evenly, his gaze trying to remind the big man what was at stake.

And then they were off.

They drove to the site in a Lincoln Town Car exactly like the one they'd used the last time, parking at a much smaller building in the middle of a large, unobstructed field. As they approached, they'd seen movement all around the horizon — small flickers in every direction. Somehow, they'd been surrounded. But that made sense and was even okay with Reginald, seeing as the humans were already holding all of the cards.

Lafontaine and a human guard were already there,

already out of their car and waiting, their headlights on and pointing toward the vampires. Reginald could see a shape in the back of the car that had to be Timken. There was also a fourth man in the group, unarmed and unarmored, wearing a tattered suit. He approached Reginald, who'd been driving, and held out his hand. Reginald, guessing, gave him the keys. The man climbed into the Town Car behind them, started it, and drove away. The move struck Reginald as funny, but he decided not to comment. Instead, he looked at Lafontaine and his armed escort across the parking lot, then at Claude.

"I'm glad you understand the need to help the Vampire Nation resolve this," said Claude. "Despite... you know."

"If you talk to me again," said Reginald, "I will try to kill you. I'm sure I'll fail and you'll kill me instead, but then you'll be short one fat genius brain."

Reginald was sure that Claude would retort — was almost hoping he would — but the big man only looked at Reginald and then closed his mouth with a sense of "fair enough."

Lafontaine, who hadn't bothered with his sunglasses this time, dragged the shape from the back seat and began walking with it toward the center of the parking lot, backlit by the other car's headlights. The guard followed on Lafontaine's other side. As they came nearer, Reginald could see Timken's face. His hair was disheveled but he looked otherwise pristine, almost ready for a photo shoot.

Then they stopped, and Reginald suddenly realized that nobody would be entering the building. The exchange would be conducted in the open. That, too, made sense, but Reginald couldn't help but look over at the building, wondering if it was filled with human snipers.

Lafontaine beckoned. Reginald and Claude walked forward to join them.

Right now, all of the humans at the besieged blood farms would be lining up at the gates. The vampire troops guarding the gates would be allowing them to do so, lowering their weapons. It was all being televised by news crews, and the whole nation was watching. That, Reginald thought, was the hidden reason behind this exchange — the reason Lafontaine had insisted on it. It wasn't just about freeing the captive humans; it was about changing hearts and minds. The public would see the Vampire Nation regain its leader, but it would also see the Nation allow 75 percent of its blood supply walk away unmolested. The surrender of sustenance would demoralize the vampire world to the point of breaking while simultaneously giving the humans unbridled new levels of hope. In the minds of the watching humans, the righteous would have won. Their cause would have become not just *possible*... but really just a matter of time.

On his belt, Claude wore a cell phone. This was intended to be straightforward; Claude would use the phone to tell the vampire troops to allow the humans to pass the gates, then Lafontaine would hand Timken over, and then when the blood stock was safely away, Lafontaine would order his troops to retreat. But until those events actually took place, anything could happen. There were guns aimed in every direction, creating a giant Mexican standoff.

Reginald had stopped caring. All that mattered were Claire and Nikki, ideally Brian, and, if possible, himself. That was it. As he stood in the dark, headlight-lit parking lot, he realized that he didn't care about the humans of the world; he didn't care about the vampires of the world; he didn't even care about the human community where his mother and Nikki's sister had lived and died, or the cluster of vampires he knew back at home. In an ideal world, everyone would live. Maybe they'd join hands and sing and braid flowers through each other's hair. But that wasn't going to happen, and he just *didn't care.* Nikki. Claire. Maybe Brian. Maybe himself. And the rest could go to Hell.

They stopped ten feet from Lafontaine, Timken, and the guard. Timken was at the end of what appeared to be a silver-chain leash. Claude picked up the phone, dialed a number, and put the phone on speaker. They heard Ophelia's voice.

"The gates are open," she said, her voice distorted by the phone's speaker. "The humans are lined up, the guards awaiting your command."

"How do the humans look?" said Claude. "For the cameras, I mean?"

"Clean and unabused enough. But a lot of them still look sick."

"Good," said Claude. "Stand by."

"Standing by, sir."

Claude looked up from the phone and met Timken's eyes.

"How are you, Mr. President?" he said. Reginald couldn't help looking over. Hearing concern come out of Claude's mouth was surreal. He tried again to pry into Claude's thoughts, but Claude still had his impervious wall up.

"Oh, peachy," said Timken.

Reginald looked at Lafontaine. He was dressed in dirty blue jeans and an old button-up shirt that was whole but well-worn. As before, his empty eyes were looking directly at Reginald and Claude as if he could see them, and Reginald again wondered how. The guard, beside him, was carrying a weapon with a tank under the barrel like a giant squirt gun, but Lafontaine himself was unarmed. Still,

Reginald remembered what had happened last time. He thought of the glints they'd seen on the horizon. The unknown element of the building beside them. And Lafontaine's dark skin, which might again have been covered in the vampire disease agent. They were ready for anything, appearances to the contrary.

"I've been watching the news while we've been waiting," said Lafontaine. Then he nodded with satisfaction. "It looks like you're keeping up your end of the bargain on the blood farms."

"We don't really have a choice," said Claude, a scowl forming on his face.

"Sure you do. You could let him die."

Claude shook his head, exasperated.

Lafontaine turned to assess the president as if he'd never seen him with his sightless eyes before, starting at his feet and scanning him upward. Then he turned back to Claude and Reginald.

"I shouldn't let him go," he said. "I've heard the stories about vampires from my grandmother's day. You used to stay in the shadows. You hid, before anyone knew you even existed. But this one right here —" He shook Timken's chain. "— was the one who made you come out. He's the one who planned the slaughter of humanity."

"Well," said Claude, "him and me."

Lafontaine was looking at Timken again. He sighed. "Well," he said, "a deal is a deal." He locked eyes with Claude, then with the others. He paused. Then he said, "Do I need to remind you that if you try anything, we'll kill you all?"

Claude laughed.

Lafontaine ignored the insult. "And do I need to remind you that if you think you can kill *us*, you're sorely mistaken?"

This time, Claude didn't break a smile.

"And while we're at it, I'll just go ahead and remind you that we've watched you since you rolled out of New York, since you took that wrong turn seventeen miles back and had to turn around. We've got eyes in the sky, and eyes all around. Enough to be sure that you don't have anyone waiting to jump on us this time."

"Fine," said Claude.

Lafontaine nodded. "Then go ahead and do your part."

Claude looked down at the phone in his hand. "General Thax?" he said.

"Yes, sir?"

"Release the humans."

"Yes, sir."

They stood for a moment, everyone staring at each other. Claude started to talk, but Lafontaine held up a finger. He looked over at the guard beside him. The guard touched an earpiece, listened, and then nodded. Then Lafontaine carefully, using only his fingertips, lifted the silver chain from around Timken's neck.

"Wouldn't want to touch his skin with mine and kill him by accident," he said, noticing Reginald's gaze. Then he laughed. "Well... at least not yet."

The chain came off. Lafontaine nodded at Timken. The guard raised his weapon and trained it on the president's back, casually, just in case. Claude watched the display, seething. But something was wrong; Claude was too tense. Something had gone sour. They needed to finish this and get out.

Timken walked the short distance and came to stand beside Claude. He straightened his suit coat.

"You okay, sir?" said Claude.

Timken nodded. "I'm fine."

Then Claude looked directly at Lafontaine, grasped Timken's head between his hands, and twisted it off his neck.

"Now," he growled, "you have nothing to hold against us."

Timken's body had begun to spark. Claude shoved it hard at the guard. Timken's corpse, now flaming, struck the guard like a two-hundred-pound sack of flour, driving him to the ground. The guard's head racked hard on the concrete of the parking lot, and then he began to burn.

Claude had dropped the phone when he'd decapitated Timken. He stooped to pick it up.

"General Thax," he said, "tell the farm guards to kill the humans."

"Sir?"

He raised his eyes to stare at Lafontaine. "Do it."

Claude pocketed the phone, then marched slowly toward the human.

"Stay back!" he said, raising his hands. "I'm contaminated!"

"Oh, don't worry," said Claude, a smile surfacing beneath his black goatee. "I won't kill you. I want to be sure you're able to see them die."

140

TWELVE

Evil

Reginald was shell-shocked. Of all the ways the exchange could have unfolded, this was the one he hadn't seen coming. But after Lafontaine ran from the parking lot to his presumably waiting troops, Claude turned and marched unhurriedly past the burning guard, stopping just long enough to drive his boot into the man's face and end his misery. Then he began to walk back the way they'd come without a word. Reginald, after a pregnant moment, followed. He was in a dream. What would happen now? And how had he — Reginald Baskin, protector of Nikki and Claire — failed them all?

Claude waited for Reginald to catch up. The humans, who'd obviously been watching, were already descending on the parking lot and the running figure of Walter Lafontaine. Reginald came up beside the new president and looked over, feeling that if he'd never done it before, he was now looking into the face of pure evil. Claude didn't turn. Reginald found himself no longer angry at the big man. He couldn't be angry because he felt so many

141

other emotions in anger's place: disbelief, terror, ejected from reality.

The whole game had changed in the span of thirty seconds. Anything could happen now. He could imagine the blood farm guards gunning down the retreating humans, wasting bullets and lives and stock, decimating the blood supply through the Nation's own volition. Reginald could almost understand if Claude had sacrificed Timken in the Vampire Nation's best interests, as Timken had always seemed to think he was doing. But if that was Claude's intention, wouldn't he have recaptured the humans instead of executing them? Now the Nation would be just as short on blood as if they'd gone free — but now, the humans would be twenty times more driven to unleash everything they had.

"You've killed us all," Reginald said, his mouth wanting to hang open.

The humans turned as they descended, driving their vehicles and sprinting toward Reginald and Claude. Reginald could see the glint of gunsights, could hear the first firing of shells.

But milliseconds later, Claude half-squatted and grabbed Reginald's left calf, casually straightening up and dropping Reginald onto his back with a thud. Then the world became a blur of dust and pain as Claude ran, dragging Reginald behind him. Reginald could feel his skull opening, could feel the skin ripping off his back.

It went on forever. Reginald let his mind go, turning inside, finally finding voluntary control of his internal pain switch — or maybe just rediscovering traumatic shock. But then sometime later, he was thrown roughly through the door of the USVC building's loading bay, left to bleed and heal in a pile on the floor. Claude didn't bother with pleasantries once he'd delivered Reginald like so much incoming freight. He blurred away, and then Reginald was alone.

Reginald ran upstairs to find Nikki, Claire, and Brian. He didn't need to tell them what had happened. They knew that the humans had been executed; they'd watched it unfold live on VNN. They hadn't, however, known that Timken had been killed, though they'd assumed from what they'd seen publicly that the deal had gone bad. The propaganda machine, however, was already hard at work, trying to turn the slaughter of the blood stock into some kind of a necessity, or possibly even a victory.

"He's done," said Nikki. "They'll lynch him. His own people."

Reginald shook his head. "They won't. There's only room for one enemy in the public eye, and right now, the bigger enemy is the humans."

"But Claude…"

"… will be the man in charge when the dust settles, if it ever does. And the vampires of the world will become convinced that whatever happened at the farms *had* to be done once Claude explains how the humans killed the president."

"Nobody will fall for that," said Brian.

Reginald turned to his brother with a small smile. "I wish I could still believe that," he said.

Reginald demanded that they leave, and nobody argued. He began packing the room, barking at Nikki and Brian to do the same. Claire, who'd only brought a back-pack, followed them around in turns, sticking mostly with Reginald because he moved at a speed she could keep up with. They had the room cleared in just over a minute.

Once they were packed, they trotted to the elevator. They began moving upward. Then the elevator shuddered to a stop, and the emergency lights went on. It could be

Claude clamping them down and trying to keep them in place, or it could be that the power was out, that the US Vampire Council building had finally fallen under the weight of the human population of New York.

Reginald shoved Claire to the front of the elevator. Claire looked over her shoulder once, but he only nodded. She put her hand against the panel, and the elevator's overhead light immediately lit and the box began to move. It reached the top floor, and Reginald nodded at Claire again to take the lead. She did, taking them to the stairwell and then to the roof, where the sky overhead was gray, still glowing from below with the lights of the city. The helicopter was still where Claire had left it, landed askew like the world's worst aerial parking job. Reginald wanted to crack a joke to loosen the mood, but before he could, on the street far below, they saw an explosion of bright light — a bit of ultraviolet flash preceding a conventional explosion as the wall around the protected section of the city was breached. And perhaps, Reginald thought, that bomb had been a dirty one. Why not? Maybe they'd even made their biological weapon airborne by now. They had the brains and the vampires were forty years out of practice. And the humans, who owned the day and the open land, were slowly buying themselves all the time they'd ever need.

The helicopter lifted off under Claire's touch, and the chopper full of vampires began lumbering through the sky over Manhattan. Reginald half expected artillery to bring them down, but there was too much excitement and light and fire below; neither the humans nor vampires were concerned about one lone helicopter out about its business. The thundering of the rotors was deafening. The ride was jarring; they kept pitching up and down, lurching either with the breeze or under Claire's inexpert piloting. He wished he could fly without assistance — just fly through the breeze like a bird or Superman. Maurice had flown, once, when he'd come to save Reginald and die in the doing. But what had Brian said? That the vampire agent was like human adrenaline, that it responded in times of extreme duress to give vampires strength and new abilities. But how was that possible? Nobody knew. The very thing that made them *them*, and nobody knew anything about it. Was it a germ? A virus? Reginald had asked, but the reactions he always got were almost perplexed. How could anyone know such a thing? And really, why would anyone care?

Curiosity wasn't a problem for humans, and it had never ceased being present in Reginald when he'd turned. So why was *that?* But that, too, was something nobody seemed to know.

They crossed the sky in their giant mechanical bird, a middle-aged woman who looked like a college student piloting the craft without knowing how she was doing it. Reginald wondered if Claire had thought to check the gas, then wondered if it mattered. Could she turn the rotors herself? Could she run the engine? Could she make sparks in the cylinders, driving the pistons by the force of mental incendiaries? But ultimately it didn't matter; they made it back and unloaded, leaving the copter at the converted hospital where Claire had found it. Then they located the car she'd taken, found it blessedly dayproofed, and drove into the wilds, into a thicket, and waited for the daylight to arrive.

THIRTEEN

Made

"Put it right there, fatass," said Maurice, pointing Reginald to a spot where he could slot another piece into the codex puzzle.

Inside Reginald's mind — his brain working as his body slept in the shielded, dayproofed car — he sat his imaginary self on a chair. The room around him became a study, responding to his mental desire to have a studious discussion. Then he said, "I'm not a fatass, Maurice."

"Really."

"Really. I'm Reginald Baskin. You're Maurice Toussant. Or at least, you were. I'm not fat and I'm not white and you don't have the acne of a teenager. I'm not a vampire and you're not a vampire. We're just Reginald and Maurice."

Reginald's mental projection of Maurice sat in an imaginary leather chair across from Reginald's. "This is fascinating," he said.

"Nobody wants to see Reginald, except for Nikki and Claire. They all want me for what they think I am. But I'm not those things. I'm more than those things."

"But you are also those things, Reginald," said Maurice.

"I refuse to be defined as fat. I refuse to be defined as a mastermind, or a strategist. I *definitely* refuse to be defined as a leader, as Claire said once upon a time that I was supposed to be. And I also refuse to be defined as a vampire or a human. I hate both of them. I want out. I want to be my own thing."

"I see. And how do you plan to do that?"

"I'll stay in here," Reginald said. "In here — and nowhere else — I am only Reginald. I am only myself, and nothing else."

Maurice leaned forward and poked Reginald in his big imaginary gut like the Pillsbury Dough Boy. "Then tell me," he said, "why are you still fat in here?"

Reginald looked down, seeing his imagined body with his internal eyes. He hadn't thought about that.

Maurice continued. "Do I have to point out that I'm actually mostly *you*, and that hence it is *you* who keeps calling you 'fatass?' Do I have to point out that if *you* are *you* in here and nothing else, then it is *you* who has chosen to present *you* to *yourself* as a fat vampire?"

As if on cue, Reginald's fangs popped out. He put his hand over his mouth.

"You are who you are, Reginald. The decision you have to make isn't whether you are going to be what and who you are, but whether you can accept it. And this?" He gestured out at the mostly assembled vampire codex, which was inexplicably still visible through the wall even though they'd sat down in a mental study. "This tells *all* of us who we *all* are. Only *you* could solve this puzzle. You understand that, right? After forty years of living with this puzzle in your head, that *has* finally sunk in, hasn't it?"

Reginald shrugged. "I guess."

"Then that means that you really *are* a kind of Chosen One. Nobody wants to think about that — especially the Chosen Ones themselves, because it sounds so douchey — but it's true. Only, you weren't really *chosen*. You were *made*. You were a statistical eventuality. Nobody handpicked you to decipher the codex. The codex was always there in plain sight. That piece in your hand? I could have noticed that particular memory when I was alive. Hell, it's from my own memories! And I had access to the thoughts of my maker to some degree, so there are other pieces I could have seen. But only you, who were special enough to see it all, could have put the entire puzzle together."

"Because Balestro gave me that blast back in Germany," said Reginald. "If he hadn't done that, I wouldn't be able to see the entire vampire bloodline. And if I couldn't see the bloodline, I couldn't put it all together."

"True," said Maurice. "But Balestro only *chose* you after you were already here. Maybe he gave you the ability to bloodwalk after he realized who you already were — that you were the only mind ever created that could have seen order in all of these memories... that could have looked through all of that vampire history and seen the pattern in it."

Reginald felt exasperated. Something had bothered him from the very beginning, but he hadn't yet verbalized it even inside his own head. It came out now, as he looked across the codex puzzle and saw how close it was to completion — how close this whole adventure was to being over, for better or for worse.

"But *why*, Maurice?" he asked. "Why did Balestro give me that ability at all? What did he want from me? The angels never came back. Timken and Claude took that to mean that vampires had done their job, that no news from angels was good news. But I don't buy it. I think that whatever they wanted from us — from the whole world, maybe — isn't finished."

Maurice shrugged. "I don't know. Which is to say that *you* don't know, and that your deductive powers, no matter how creatively you've personified them —" He put his palm on his own narrow chest. "— aren't sufficient for anything beyond a guess."

Reginald looked down at his big stomach, which was easily as big inside his own head as it was in life. It was unfair, the way even his subconscious mind insisted on beating him up.

"So what do we do?" he asked.

"You mean, what do *you* do?"

"Sure."

"You keep on. You keep building the puzzle."

Reginald looked out across the vast, endless floor. "But it's almost finished."

"Then you finish it."

"Then what?"

"You mean, what do you do next?" Maurice asked.

Reginald nodded.

"By which I mean, what do *we* do next?"

Reginald nodded again.

"I have no idea, fatass," he said.

Reginald looked at the huge cardboard puzzle piece in his hand, representing yet another datum to slot into the puzzle. He didn't precisely know what to *do*, but he realized as he looked at it that he did know what to do *next*. He would read the piece, and he'd see what fate had in store, and then he'd do it, because apparently there was no other way.

Reginald dropped the piece into the puzzle. He felt

another bit of realization dawn. It was almost complete. It was almost there.

"Maurice," he said.

Maurice looked up.

"You're not entirely me, are you? I mean, the present part of you. The part that isn't your stash of memories."

Maurice looked thoughtful. "Well, I don't know. Is a puzzle the sum of all of its pieces? Or is there something above them that transcends all of the little parts?"

"Is that a metaphysical question?" Reginald asked. But Maurice just smiled.

Reginald looked down at his metaphorical feet and saw two more metaphorical puzzle pieces. Now that the codex was mostly assembled, their position was obvious. He didn't have to think about where they went, and so he watched as they floated up and zipped into place, not crossing the space in between here and there so much as appearing where they belonged. Then the whole puzzle seemed to shimmer and shine, and Reginald felt his knowledge of it (so far, anyway) transform into an intimate familiarity with it. It was like the point in learning a language where you stopped translating words and simply started thinking in the new tongue.

And as Reginald felt himself become fluent in the vampire codex, he felt as if he were flying. All of the pieces in the larger puzzle — still metaphorical, but now outside of himself, in the bigger world — started to come together. He saw how it all fit. He began to see the truth.

Vampires and humans.

Humans and vampires.

And he saw how it all ended — which was to say how it *didn't* end, how it hung delicately from a point where the whole thing was stuck — a point past which even Reginald, with his insider's knowledge, couldn't see.

He awoke in the shielded car, feeling hot and uncomfortable. Nikki had been driving before they'd parked in the thicket, and she was still asleep beside him in the driver's seat. He reached over and turned the key, starting the engine. Then he turned on the air conditioning, amused as if for the first time that a vampire could care about the temperature — that a cold being could be bothered by heat. But reality, more than ever, was not what it had once seemed to be.

Nikki, startled by the sound of the engine, stirred. She blinked, stretched, and then looked over at Reginald.

"I know how to end it," he said.

Nikki blinked again, seemingly trying to process his words. "You do?"

"Yes," he said. "But we're going to need a little bit of help."

FOURTEEN

Car

The screen where the windshield would be on a normal, non-dayproofed car flickered. They'd turned the screens off — on all of the car's faux windows — because leaving them on while they slept made them all feel like they were out in the open. Now only the windshield was active, showing them nothing and then what looked like the inside of a hotel room. Then it was nothing again.

"Come on, Claire," Reginald mumbled, as if in prayer.

Claire, in the back seat, yawned. She focused, and the windshield flickered. Then they saw the room again in all its glory, steady as anything.

"Got it?" Reginald said, turning to look at Claire.

"I had it just fine from the beginning," she said. "I'm just tired, is all. I'm used to a vampire sleep schedule. What time is it? Like 3PM?"

Reginald didn't answer, and instead turned back to the screen. "So now what?" he said.

"Pretend it's a window," said Claire.

Reginald looked again at the room in front of him. It

was bizarre. The clarity was perfect, just like the projection of the road outside would normally have been. It looked like they were looking through a car's windshield, but the car in question had somehow plowed into a Holiday Inn.

"Where is he?"

"I'd guess the bed is behind us," said Claire.

Reginald turned around as if expecting to see the other half of the hotel room in the rear window. But instead he saw nothing, because the rest of the screens were off.

"Yell," Claire suggested.

So Reginald did. He felt stupid yelling in a car filled with four people, but he did it anyway. Shortly afterward, there was a noise from offscreen, then the sound of footsteps. The steps had a confused rhythm, as if their owner didn't know what was going on. Which was accurate.

"Go to the computer!" Reginald yelled.

The footsteps became louder. Then the view changed and Reginald found himself looking at the entirely-too-large face of Charles Barkley.

"Jesus, trim your nose hair," said Nikki.

"Reginald?" said Charles, looking confused.

"And your ear hair," Nikki added.

Charles tapped the screen. The view bounced, then was still. "How are you doing this?" he said.

"It's not important. The important thing is that…"

The image bounced again as Charles flicked the screen of his laptop back in New York. The feeling was disorienting. Before, it had felt like they'd crashed into a hotel room. Now it felt like they'd crashed into a vibrating hotel room.

"I didn't call you," said Charles, messing with his keyboard. "What is this, Skype?" He peered closer at the screen, which to everyone in the car made it look like he was peering at their feet because the camera was up higher, and he wasn't looking into it.

"Better than Skype," said Claire.

Charles kept flicking the screen. "Where are you?"

"We're in a car. Where we are isn't important."

"And you've got a wireless signal?"

"Who cares? It doesn't matter."

"How did you get out of the building? Claude was furious."

"Again, not important. Look. I need you to get Walker."

"Why?"

Brian leaned forward between the seats, his massive shoulders actually pushing the seats apart. In a loud monotone, more statement than question, he blurted, "OH MY GOD WHY ARE YOU SUCH A DOUCHEBAG." Then he leaned back.

"Why do you want Walker?"

"Because he's so charming," said Nikki.

"Because we need his help," said Reginald.

But as soon as he'd said it, he realized how stupid this idea was. Sure, Walker would know where to find Paul Isis because it was his job to know. But Walker knew Paul as the blood farm humane treatment officer, not as a member of the Underground, which was how Nikki knew him. Might Reginald's inquiry get Paul in trouble? Paul was human, allowed to live free because his work with the blood farms made for good PR, like having a dog sit on the board of a company that tested cosmetics on animals. But Paul had taken a big risk by supporting the Vampire Underground, and if Walker put two and two together now, Reginald might well be signing his death warrant.

He shook the thought aside. There was no other way. Paul was the only one who could make the contact they needed, and going through Walker was the only way to contact Paul. They'd been unable to reach him so far, but the grateful slave would forever be reachable by the man with the whip.

"Why should Walker help you?" said Charles.

"Why don't you let him decide?" Reginald retorted.

"I'm not your slave," said Charles, putting his hand somewhere above the camera. "You want Walker? Fine. Go barge into Walker's room." The view started to tilt downward. Reginald saw the laptop's keyboard approach the camera, then shouted for Charles to wait.

The view returned as Charles re-opened the computer.

"Charles, please," said Reginald. "We can't get to his screen. His computer is closed. His phone is either not with him or is off. We need you to get him for us."

"Why should I help you?" said Charles.

"Oh come on, Charles," said Brian from the backseat. "For once in your life, don't be a cliche and a cockface."

Charles rolled his eyes. Then he vanished, and a few minutes later they saw Walker's perfect teeth. The rest of his face came with them. He stood beside Charles, both vampires looking down at the screen, side by side.

Charles gestured at the screen. "Well, there they are," he said to Walker. "Have at it."

Walker instantly became Walker. He totally ignored the strangeness of the incident, the strangeness of Charles's summons, the way they'd all parted in New York, and the fact that the new homicidal president would almost certainly be on a rampage. Instead he said, "Hey Nikki. Show me your tits."

Nikki rolled her eyes.

"Seriously," he said. His voice sounded almost sad.

"Todd," said Reginald, "we need your help to…"

"Are you guys in a car?"

"Yes."

155

"How are you…?"

"Does it matter?"

"If you're in a car, you can show me your tits. Nobody's going to see."

"Gross!" said Claire. And again, Reginald remembered Claire as he'd first met her, wondering if he'd stunted her growth by being in her life, like a corpulent cigarette habit.

"This is stupid," said Charles. He turned to Walker. "Claude is looking for them. We should tell him that they're…"

Brian leaned forward again, pushing the seats apart with his hugeness. "OH MY GOD WHY ARE YOU SUCH A DOUCHEBAG," he speak-shouted.

Charles ignored Brian and kept speaking to Walker. "Seriously, Claude will shit a brick if he…"

"Charles," said Reginald, barging in and cutting him off, "what has Claude been doing?"

"Why should we tell you?"

"Look," said Reginald. "Claude killed Timken. You know that, right?"

"The humans killed Timken," said Walker, suddenly serious.

"No. Claude did it. I watched him do it. Lafontaine had released him. He came to us. Claude asked how he was. He said he was fine. Then Claude twisted his head off, knocked out Lafontaine's man, and ordered the humans at the farms shot."

"Bullshit." It was Walker, suddenly stripped of his jocularity.

"*Not* bullshit. Claude wanted the presidency from the beginning. The Annihilists want a vampire planet. Timken came close, but not close enough. There were still too many humans out there for Claude, and the way Timken handled things wasn't efficient enough throughout the entire war. I was in the Antarctic station. I saw how his V-Crews operated. I promise you both: Timken was an evil son of a bitch, but Claude makes Timken look like Santa. Jesus, Walker, don't be a punk for once in your life. Open your eyes. Surely you've seen how he is?"

Walker shook his head. "Bullshit."

Reginald realized that he shouldn't have taken the tangent when it had opened. Now he'd gotten Walker defensive — and Reginald had never, *ever* known Walker to admit being wrong. Walker didn't "get" civility; he'd never understood that there were other people in the world and that he wasn't the only one. He had a very selective memory and felt the need to twist reality so that it agreed with the way he acted. If humans took over and reestablished order and Walker somehow survived, he'd suddenly decide that he'd been turned against his will. But the most frightening thing of all was that it wouldn't be a lie; inside of Walker's own mind, he'd believe it to be true.

Now that Reginald had raised Walker's defenses, what were the chances he'd help them contact Paul Isis, who might be able to reach Lafontaine? It wasn't something they could afford to trifle with. If anyone had his finger on the trigger right now, it was Walter Lafontaine. And if he pulled that trigger, then everyone would pay.

"Look," Reginald told him. "It doesn't matter. I need you to put us in touch with someone."

"Why?" Reginald noticed without surprise that Walker hadn't led with "who."

Reginald sighed, then decided to change tacks. "Because I think we can stop all of this."

"How are you going to do that?" Charles demanded.

Reginald locked eyes with Walker, ignoring Charles. Walker was the man whose help he needed. He couldn't feel his emotions. He was too far away. If Reginald went inside himself, he'd be able to access all of Walker's blood memories, of course, but that wouldn't help him right here and now.

"Hey Todd," he said. "How are things outside?"

"Rough but holding," he said.

"How much longer do you think you can hold out at USVC?"

"We're fine," said Charles.

But Reginald wasn't interested in Charles's opinion. Again he stared at Walker. "What do you think, Todd?"

Walker looked down. He seemed tired, as if he just wanted it all to go away. If they were under siege by the humans from the outside and under siege by Claude from the inside (for any number of imagined infractions; Claude seemed to have broken, and Reginald guessed that he'd strike at anyone who crossed him these days), then they would be worn thin indeed.

When Walker looked back up, Reginald saw that it was all true. Walker had been a jackass when they'd worked together; then he'd become a murderer; then he'd become a bloodthirsty social climber. Over and over and over, when he'd heard Walker updates in the press over the years, Reginald had wished that Nikki had just let Maurice kill him on the day of his vampire birth. But she hadn't, and now he was in their way — and simultaneously their only reluctant hope.

"It's bad, Reggie," said Walker, his voice uncharacteristically low. "But I'm sure as hell not going to help you and make it worse."

"Worse how?"

"By pissing off Claude. We're stuck here with him, and for now, there's no way out. Ophelia has been giving us battlefield reports. Whenever they send troops in, the humans descend on them with that black plague shit. It makes them impossible to touch. They blew a kind of dirty bomb just after you and Claude came back, and it killed a lot of the guards outside the building. We've heard the same thing from other cities, but it's hard to say because they've done something to our communications. I don't suppose you've checked the VNN feed today?"

Reginald turned to Claire. She shook her head side to side, but her hooded eyes conveyed the message perfectly well: she wasn't saying "no" meaning that she hadn't seen the feed. She was saying "no" to indicate that she'd seen it (or absorbed it, or plucked it from the air) just fine... and that there was something wrong with it.

Walker saw Claire's head shake and nodded at her. "Right. It's in and out. Mostly out. We don't know what's happening in Geneva or anywhere else, although we did manage to receive a message from your buddy Karl Stromm in Europe, who says they're bunkered in like we are. But it looks like the humans might have blown other bombs in other places. And there's something else. Rumor says that..."

Charles shot him a look. "That's bullshit," he said to Walker.

Walker shook Charles off and continued. "Some people on Fangbook — when you can access Fangbook, I mean — are saying that the humans are drinking it. The plague shit, I mean. Vampires are afraid to feed on wild humans."

Nikki turned to Reginald. "Jesus," she said.

"It's a lie," said Charles. "It would kill them if they drank it."

"It doesn't kill them when it's on their skin," said Brian from behind.

Reginald looked back at Walker. "Look. I've got to talk to Lafontaine."

"Well, good luck with that," said Walker.

"I think Paul Isis can contact him for us."

"Us?" said Charles.

Walker was shaking his head. "Why would Paul be able to contact him?"

Reginald looked at Nikki. Nikki didn't want to shake her head, but her eyes told him not to say why.

"I just think he can. He's human, after all."

"Oh, and all humans know each other?" said Charles.

"Just… do you know where he is?"

Walker shrugged. "Well, communications are down," he said. But it wasn't a categorical denial. Reginald saw a hole opening in the fence.

"But you know how to contact him," said Reginald. "You do, don't you?"

"I really don't understand why Paul would…"

"Just… do you know how to find him or not?"

"He has a cell. We had to contact him a lot while he was out on farm visits. But that guy is such a little prick. He's…"

"Call him."

"I don't see what good that would…"

"Walker," said Reginald, switching away from the familiar use of his first name. "Just do it."

Walker looked at the screen for a long time. Charles's gaze went back and forth between the man next to him and the computer screen. Finally he took Walker by the shoulder and turned him away from the camera, then pulled him back a few steps, out of range. Reginald watched all he could see of them (the tops of their heads) while Charles hissed something to Walker and Walker hissed back. Then Walker returned to the computer. In the background, Charles was whispering into a phone. Maybe — hopefully — to Paul Isis. Although why Charles would have anything to do with Paul was beyond Reginald.

"You really think you can stop this, Reggie?"

"Reginald," Reginald corrected. "And the answer is that I'd like to try."

"Lafontaine isn't going to want to talk to you even if Paul can somehow connect you. This is strike three. Two meetings, two betrayals. I watched helmetcam video of the first one, where Timken tried to fuck them and they fucked him right back. I don't know who fucked who the second time, but it ended up with our guy dead and a lot of their people dead. He's not going to trust you any further than he can throw you." Then, because he was Walker, he said, "And just look at you, Reggie. Nobody's throwing you anywhere."

"Let me worry about that."

"Fine," said Walker. He pulled a phone from his pocket, then clicked around. "You ready?"

Reginald realized Walker wasn't going to make the call. He was going to give them Paul's mobile number. He probably didn't want to get in the middle. With Claude breathing down his neck, he didn't want to be arranging anything Claude might not approve of. If Reginald got ahold of Isis's number, though, then Walker couldn't be held responsible for what Reginald decided to do with it.

Nikki had a scrap of paper and a pen. "Go."

Walker read the number. Nikki copied it down, then read it back to confirm. Reginald let her do it, knowing she'd want to do it as an act of assistance. But Reginald, with his databank mind, didn't need her note, and he didn't need anyone to repeat anything. Now that he'd seen the completed vampire codex, he really only needed one thing, and that thing was approaching faster than he wanted it to.

"One more thing," said Walker, just as they were about to hang up.

"What?"

"Before Timken took over, your buddy was Deacon, right?"

Reginald took a deep breath. "My maker was. Yes."

"And you were his Vice Deacon."

"Yes."

"And he's dead now."

Reginald stuffed down irritation. This was Walker at his classic best. He probably wasn't even trying to be an asshole. He just couldn't help it.

"Yes."

"But if he'd died all those years ago, when you were Vice, then you would be in charge now. Instead of Claude."

"That's a hell of a leap," said Reginald. In reality the answer was "not a chance," because Reginald would have been overthrown just as Maurice had been, and it would have been far easier. Charles might or might not have seized power for himself afterward, and Timken may or may not have swooped in to save/doom the day. But most of all, even if Reginald *had* found himself in the Deacon's (or president's) seat, he would have abdicated immediately. He wasn't a leader, and didn't remotely want to be.

Except, he realized, that's exactly what he was doing right now: leading. But so much had changed.

"You think you're better than Claude, though. Right?"

It was Nikki who answered. Reginald wanted to dodge the question, but she took it like a tackle.

"He is," she said.

"Well, for what it's worth," said Walker, looking quiet

and thoughtful, "thank God that didn't happen, because you really would have fucked it up."

The laptop lid snapped shut and Charles's computer, in New York, went to sleep.

"When we're done trying to save the world," said Brian from the back seat, "I'd like to pull that guy's asshole over his head."

FIFTEEN

Hero

Reginald stepped out of the car when the sun was fully set. Nikki stepped out with him. They'd driven for two hours, into New York's upstate, over a hundred miles from where Timken had been killed. Nikki reached out and took Reginald's hand, then held it to her cheek.

"This is the part where I tell you not to go," she said.

"This is the part where I say, like a cliche, that I have to go."

"And then this," she said, "is where I try again."

Reginald looked through the still-open door. Brian had emerged from the car's other side and was standing with an enormous forearm on the hood, but Claire was still sitting inside, fiddling with something.

"I suppose it won't work if I tell you that you have to stay to protect Claire," said Reginald, "seeing as she's nearing retirement age."

Nikki shook her head. "No." She let Reginald's arm hang, his hand still clasped in hers. "But I understand."

"Do you?"

"Sure. Do you remember the story you told me about

164

the night you were turned? Maurice suggested that you be the first person in history to actually believe what he was seeing, instead of playing through the tired old 'vampires don't exist and I'm not a vampire OMG' trope." She actually said all three letters: *Oh-em-gee.*

"I remember."

"Well, I'd love to be the first companion in history to see that there really is no other way."

Reginald smiled.

"There isn't, is there?"

Instead of giving her the answer she already knew, he asked another. "Is that what you are? A 'companion'?"

"I think that's how Raymond Burr referred to his gay lover: '*Companion.*'"

"I am a lot like Raymond Burr," said Reginald, imagining himself with a beard.

"In this scenario," said Nikki, "*I'm* Raymond Burr."

"Hot," said Reginald.

Reginald looked off into the distance. The expanse he had to walk was, by design, entirely treeless. Lafontaine had wanted nothing to do with Reginald when Paul had arranged their phone call on Nikki's pleading request. It had taken a lot of threats (from Lafontaine) and begging (from Reginald) before Lafontaine would even consider it. It was only when Reginald hinted at the idea of the codex and its revelation that Lafontaine began to listen. He waffled for a long time, saying that he'd looked up the fat vampire after being betrayed by him twice ("Not by me," Reginald clarified) and that he wanted to believe him, but that he wouldn't be a fool three times. Reginald told him that he just wanted to be heard. It had to be in person, because the human mastermind needed to use whatever eyeless eyes he had to look Reginald in the face and see the truth: that they were more alike than different. By "they,"

Reginald had meant vampires and humans, but he realized
quickly that Lafontaine was thinking of himself and Reginald — the fat human and the fat vampire. And as strange
and stupid of a bond as that was, Lafontaine had seemed
to understand.

So they'd agreed to meet for the third time — just the
two of them, on decidedly unequal ground.

In the middle of an old baseball field in the middle of
a maintained park, with open lines of sight in all
directions.

And Reginald would come alone.

Unarmed, and wearing no armor of any kind.

And the humans would come in force, armed to the
teeth.

And Reginald would find himself in a hundred
gunsights at once. And be bound in silver on arrival.

And Lafontaine would be covered in the disease agent.

And while the meeting would need to happen at night,
the humans would make sure the field lights ("not UV,"
Lafontaine said in the spirit of granting a great concession)
had power, and were on… and they'd turn half of the
lights around, to watch the surrounding area, with visibility
for miles.

And the men with the guns would be wearing night
vision goggles, prepared to annihilate anything that moved.

"It's okay," Reginald told Nikki, now holding both of
her hands in his. "I have a secret plan to overwhelm
them."

Nikki laughed. They had, of course, run through
scenario after scenario during the drive, trying to find holes
in Lafontaine's plan. There were none. Even if they were
on good terms with the Vampire Council or CPC — which
they definitely were not — they wouldn't be able to
summon their help. The new human weapons were supe-

rior to anything the vampires had and they'd be able to see them coming a mile away. The best an armed force would be able to manage would be a full-out assault, from all directions at once. But as things stood, they were just three vampires and a mostly-human woman, so leaving three behind wasn't decreasing their impossible odds any, and Nikki knew it.

"What if he kills you?"

Reginald had considered it. The answer was that he didn't care. But the answer he gave to Nikki was the best lie he could manage: "I'm sure he won't."

"Sure with all of your big vampire brain?" Her voice hitched. She tried to hide it, but he could hear it plain as day. And he could feel her pain from the inside, as much as he tried to shut it out and give her her privacy. It was unbearable to feel, and unbearably indulgent given that he was the emotion's subject.

"Totally sure," he lied again.

"How are you going to get him to end it?"

"I'm gonna make him an offer he don't refuse."

Nikki looked at him askance. "Was that supposed to be Brando from *The Godfather*?"

"Actually I was going for DeNiro. When he was a new immigrant. Immigrants speak that way." But he realized he should have done Brando. He had late-Brando's body shape.

"I see."

"I'll be fine, Nikki."

But now Nikki's hitch had become a stifled sob. She choked it back, but a tear traced its way down the crease beside her nose, and seeing it broke something inside him.

"You're strong enough for this," he told her.

"No," she said. "I'm not."

"You are."

167

Another tear fell. She pressed a finger to his lips, silencing him. "Shh. This is the part where you're the strong one, and you go off into the sunset while your woman cries behind you." Then she smiled. "It's okay. Bittersweet is still sweet, in its own way." And with that, Reginald realized that he hadn't fooled her even one tiny little bit with his lies. And still, she was letting him go. Because the world was ending again, and this time it looked like it was ending for good.

"Third time's a charm," said Reginald, trying to force a smile. It wouldn't come. His own words clanged back in his mind. Although he'd meant that his third meeting with Lafontaine might yet succeed, his last thought had been about the end of them all. The first time the end of the world had approached, it had looked like the vampires were goners. The second time, it had been humans who neared extinction. And this time, barring a miracle, it would be both. Because even for armageddon, the third time was a charm.

Claire got out of the car and hugged Reginald. It was hard not to feel that her hug was too high. She was supposed to be at his waist, ten years old and wearing a coat with a giant anorak hood. How much she'd changed. How much they'd *all* changed, while not changing at all.

"Does the codex tell you whether this will work?" Claire asked him.

"No," he said. "What about you?"

Claire shook her head. "I've been seeing a fog in the distance of my mind for weeks, but it's *all* fog now. I kept expecting that as we went forward, the fog would clear. But now everything is covered — though whether it's gone or just hidden, I can't say. I can tell you about the past and I can tell you about the present. But the future?" She shrugged.

Nikki looked from one to the other. "Two fortune tellers. Zero fortune."

"It's a decision," said Claire. "The future is undetermined because it's all come down to the crucial decision. Free will and all. Ironically, that's the thing that saved you the first time."

Nikki gave Reginald a pained smile, her eyes wet. "Second time's a charm," she said.

"Maybe."

"And maybe the decision at hand is your decision to walk off. Into the humans' hands. Alone." She couldn't keep the bitterness out of her voice, and another tear fell.

He shook his head because he didn't know if that was the decision or not. But she waved it off, not wanting to hear.

Reginald felt his resolve beginning to wane. So he looked toward the horizon — funnily enough in the direction of the sunset, where the hero would go at the end of a western. He hugged Claire and said goodbye without saying goodbye, then took Brian by the hand and then pulled him into a hug and called him brother. He held Nikki tight, and kissed her deeply.

Then he walked away, feeling more alone than he ever had — in either of his two lives.

SIXTEEN

Baseball

Reginald wasn't strong or fast by vampire standards even after forty years, but after enough time bloodsucking, he'd gotten reasonably fast by human standards. He jogged the twenty miles to the park (the closest he was willing to drive, for the protection of the others) in under two hours, his belly flapping and jarring the entire time. The park itself wasn't hard to find. He only had to follow the lights — and the escort vehicle that pulled up beside him when he was five miles out and trained a light on him, aiming several automatic weapons and yelling at him not to flinch.

Soon a wash of bright light appeared on the horizon. He ran into its middle through a gauntlet of guns, like an Olympic torch-bearer running into the opening cere-monies. On the pitcher's mound of the baseball field was a metal chair. The bullhorn voice of the vehicle's driver commanded Reginald to sit in it, so he did. Five humans who weren't Walter Lafontaine came out of the darkness. Three aimed weapons while the other two (fully armored, as if Reginald were Hannibal Lecter) used padlocks brushed in liquid silver to bind him with what appeared to be solid silver chain. Even as Reginald felt the chain drag him down, weighing tons on his shoulders, he wondered at the chain itself. Nobody made solid silver chain. Had the humans melted silver jewelry and silver flatware to make it themselves? How many ancestral stashes had they had to raid to make it? What kind of facility had the process required? He continued to imagine vast underground human cities, complete with high-end biological labs, manufacturing plants, tech research facilities, and now an industrial smelter. The vampires had vastly, vastly underestimated their foes, as vampires always did. It was ironic that one of the things that defined the vampire population as predators was their tendency to turn a blind eye to the true threat of their prey.

Once Reginald was bound, the five humans retreated, still aiming their guns. More men appeared around the baseball field's edges, aiming weapons like spectators with a vested interest in the game's outcome. Reginald found himself painted in laser sights. He wanted to laugh, but doing so felt incredibly dangerous. The humans had been burned twice — and had done some burning themselves — so no trust was going to be granted until it was duly earned. All in all, Reginald didn't particularly care if they killed him. In many ways, death would be a relief... but he had to at least convey his message before he left the planet. He owed it to the others. He owed it to every human and vampire still alive, because without that message, none of them would be alive for long.

More lights came on facing the field. More lights came on facing away from the field. More troops swarmed. Reginald realized a strangely harmonious thought as he watched them: when they were armored, humans and vampires looked the same. Both species dressed in black armor, protected their necks, wore helmets... and, today, both wielded guns. Both had hate and suspicion in their eyes, even when their eyes weren't visible. He was watching human rebels, but they could be vampire members of the CPC. Or Timken's pre-war Sedition Army troops. Or pre-war human AVT. Or Claude's murderous, black ops V-Crews.

Killers, in the end, were killers.

And then, strangely, Reginald realized something else. Something he hadn't seen before. Not only did they look alike; they *felt* alike as well. Sitting on the chair in the middle of the brightly lit baseball field, alone and waiting to see if Lafontaine would show or if they'd kill him out of hand, Reginald realized that *he could feel the humans.* They felt like a haze of nerves, of distrust and fear and anger and focused, desperate hope. He'd always been gifted at glamouring humans, but he'd never been able to feel them before. Yet right here and now, all of that emotion and thought surrounded him like a cold fog. Maybe other vampires couldn't evolve, and maybe the angels had been right. But Reginald had never stopped evolving, never stopped discovering new talents. It should be worth something. But somehow, it never had been.

A shadow emerged from the dugout. It walked ten feet toward Reginald, still not even to home plate on the baseball field. The figure was larger than the others, wearing armor that made its chest look big. But its chest was already large. The big belly of the human — so like Reginald's big belly — was a silhouette against the blinding lights.

"I wanted to believe you, Reginald," said the shadow.

It took a few more steps, now nearing home plate.

"But you just can't be trusted, can you? I don't like the idea of killing you all. I really don't, honest. But you vampires are like killer bees. You give us no choice; we

172

can't live with you off to the side — live and let live — because every time we try to give you the benefit of the doubt, you do something to break whatever trust there almost was, and to take away the doubt."

Reginald tried to straighten his back under the chain. He looked at the fat black silhouette and said, "You're right. I'm coming at you right now. Look out; I'm dangerous."

Lafontaine's silhouette turned and yelled something into the dugout. A new silhouette emerged, holding a second silhouette. More men with weapons appeared, now pointing at Reginald and at the new figures. More lights began to scan the distance.

Reginald realized what he was looking at. Then Nikki's voice said, "I'm okay!"

Reginald wanted to scream. She'd followed him. Of *course* she'd followed him. His love for her and his fear for her were temporarily overrun by his frustration with her. She'd never trusted him to lead, and she'd never trusted him to be able to take care of himself. It was sweet until it wasn't sweet; it was kind until it was flat-out dangerous. Had she really thought she could sneak in? They'd been over this for the entire drive. There were no holes in Lafontaine's plan. The only way to meet the force in the park would be to go in heavy, with hundreds of soldiers. They didn't *have* hundreds of soldiers. They had four ordinary folks, and only two of them were any good in a fight. The idea of this whole thing had been to concede, to be humble, and to try to use brains above brawn. Reginald was never supposed to *win* this confrontation. Even the best-case scenario would be neutral. He was supposed to roll over and expose his belly, content to die so long as he could convey the truth he needed to convey. But now, Nikki had made that impossible. All that her lack of trust had done was to make sure that Reginald couldn't even roll over and be heard. She hadn't saved him, and she hadn't saved herself. And now everyone, everywhere, was going to die.

"Jesus fucking Christ, Nikki," he said. Then, knowing it was a betrayal and hating himself for it, he yelled, "I didn't know she was coming! I told her not to come!" The words felt horrible passing his lips, but the time had come for desperate measures. He and Nikki were goners anyway. He had to do what he could to salvage anything that could be salvaged.

Lafontaine walked closer. Nikki's captor held her where she was. Reginald could hear the jingle of silver chains around her shoulders and arms.

"What was the plan?" said Lafontaine. "Were you going to kill me? Was she going to sneak up behind me and bite my head off?"

Reginald felt seconds slipping away, felt blood leaking through the world's cracks. "No!" he shouted.

The human shook his head. "When I first saw you, I was shocked. I'd never seen a vampire like you. My grandfather told me that vampires are like animals. They kill their own kind. Grandpa said that vampires are pure survival of the fittest. They'll only turn thin, strong, and fast humans and will drain the rest." He gestured at his own body. "Maybe I'd have joined you once upon a time. But I figured yours was a club that wouldn't have me."

He started to pace, his shadow washed out by the multi-directional glow of the field lights and the supplementary spotlights.

"Of course, spending my whole life under the thumb of your superiority, being fed on, being treated like slaves... well, that turned me off to the idea pretty quickly, and by the time I was twelve and my beloved grandfather was killed by a blood farm guard for stealing tools to make me a toy — just one toy for the boy who grew up with an IV in his arm — I'd pretty much decided that if I ever became a vampire, the first thing I'd do would be to kill my maker. Then I'd kill the next vampire I could find, and then the next, and then the next until they killed me. And years later when I escaped, I vowed that I'd see the planet wiped clean of you or die trying. But I'd never again be your... your *food*."

He walked up to Reginald and stood in front of him. He squatted, surprisingly agile for a big man.

"But you? You weren't like the others — and honestly, the fact that you are who you are is the reason I'm even here tonight. I saw you in that first melee. You reacted like a human. You're slow. You're weak. You were afraid. I can tell the others don't even respect you. It's in the way they look at you..."

Reginald stopped him, unable to help himself. It was Lafontaine's mention of "looking" that did it.

"What happened to your eyes?" he said.

A small, surprised smile crawled onto Lafontaine's dark lips. He pointed at Reginald. "And that's another thing about you, Reginald Baskin: you're *curious*. I've never met another vampire who was curious. Our scientists have tried to figure that out — to understand your psychology — but it's hard. Vampires don't tend to be cooperative when we catch them and try to test them, and when we remove your brains to autopsy them, they turn to ash. We had to study your blood while you were still alive with it still circulating in your veins, or else we wouldn't have been able to develop our ace-in-the-hole." He ran a finger up his bare arm, presumably rubbing a line in the disease agent on his skin. "But it's not just curiosity that most vampires lack. I've never seen a vampire who appears embarrassed, or self-conscious, or shy. But you have all of that. You hide behind the others, yet you do things that are selfless. You think beyond yourself. We've discovered the bond between maker and made, though we don't understand it, and we've watched V change under our microscopes when a maker's progeny is in danger…"

"V?" said Reginald.

"That's what we call the organism in your blood."

"What is it?" said Reginald, suddenly forgetting that he was bound, in a hundred gun sights, and that Nikki was being held captive. This was the question he'd asked his own kind over and over and never gotten an answer to. It was so strange to think that his curiosity about himself might, in his final hours, be sated by a human.

Lafontaine's strange little smile became larger and again he pointed at Reginald.

"See? There's that curiosity again. To answer your question (because I've got an investigative mind myself, and because you're not going anywhere), it looks like a virus. Not quite alive and not quite not dead. It's almost *un*dead, like you."

"A virus?"

He nodded. "And to answer your other question, I lost my eyes to cancer a few years ago, after escaping the farm. But every cloud has a sliver lining, because it makes me impervious to your little mind tricks."

"But you can see."

Lafontaine touched a small device pinned to his earlobe that Reginald had taken for an earring. "Sonar," he said. "Like a bat. With a bit of training, I can see nearly as well as you can. Well… as well as a *human* can see, anyway." He sighed. "Though I do miss colors."

Behind Lafontaine, Nikki struggled. The sound of her

chains seemed to remind Lafontaine of her presences, and of what it meant.

"I wanted to hear what you had to say," he told Reginald. "But every time I try to listen to vampires, someone gets killed. But it's okay. Silver lining, see. Because you were so unique that I was beginning to question my conviction. I was afraid I might be making a mistake, and that you weren't all worth killing. And that made it hard, because you make it impossible for us to let you survive. So in a way, I'm glad that it has turned out this way. It makes me feel so much better about what we need to do."

Reginald swallowed. "Your weapon," he said. "You have a way to deliver it."

Lafontaine nodded. "Again, I don't *want* to kill all of you, Reginald. I really don't, even after your species killed my entire family after they'd gotten too old to milk for quality blood. I don't want to kill you after you killed almost every human who once walked this planet." He squatted again, his empty sockets meeting Reginald's eyes as if they were the source of his sight. "My grandfather told me that once upon a time, there were human cities so full that the sheer number of people created disease. That there were countries that limited the number of children people could have, because the Earth was too full. Was that true?"

Reginald nodded. "It's true."

Lafontaine stood. "It's an amazing thing to think of, all those people. I've seen the old bibles: 'Go forth and multiply,' they said. We did it once. You drove us back, and now we'll have to do it again. And still, I don't want to kill anyone. But in my shoes, what would you do?" He stood, now looking down at Reginald. "I'm told that your logical mind is unmatched. So I'm actually asking: what would *you* do, if there was an intelligent, vengeful group who wanted

to kill you and suck you dry, who would hunt you forever
and never relent? You'd have to eradicate them, wouldn't
you? You wouldn't have any choice, if you wanted your
own kind to survive, but to kill them all."

Reginald found himself recalling his encounter with
Timken all those years ago. So much was the same
between that meeting and this one. Reginald had been in a
jail cell, held in place by silver. Timken had been asking
Reginald's opinion on a difficult decision, plumbing him
for input. Like Lafontaine, Timken hadn't wanted to do
what he felt needed to be done... but what choice was
there?

"I understand," said Reginald.

Lafontaine turned to the guard holding Nikki. He
gestured with his head and the solider dragged Nikki
forward. She started to say something to Reginald, to apol-
ogize, but Reginald told her with his eyes not to bother.
What was done was done. She had probably doomed them
both — had, in fact, probably doomed them all — but it
was what it was.

"Do you?" said Lafontaine. "Because I see how you
are. We have eyes everywhere. It's easy once we see how to
piggyback on vampire communications protocols — a
trick, by the way, that you used on us at the beginning, but
which we improved on — and I've been watching you,
Reginald. You and her..."

"My wife Nikki," he said. It didn't matter if Lafontaine
knew Nikki's name, but Reginald wanted to take any
opportunity he could to humanize her in Lafontaine's
mind. He was already calling Reginald by his name, and
Reginald could feel Lafontaine wanting to like him,
wanting to find a solution. His thinking of her as "Nikki"
rather than as a nameless assassin could only help.

"Well, you and Nikki and a few others seem different.

But how am I supposed to pick out the good ones from the bad ones? My first duty has to be to my species. So what can I do?"

"I know what you can do," said the guard holding Nikki, loud enough for only the two of them to hear.

The voice was familiar. And when Reginald looked up, he realized that the shape of the soldier was familiar, too. He was big, with broad shoulders.

Brian.

But when Reginald realized that his blood could almost see Lafontaine through the eyes of the vampire behind the visor, he realized that it wasn't Brian after all.

It was Claude.

SEVENTEEN

Merciless

It all clicked.

Why he could feel so much emotion at the gathering, and why he'd thought he could inexplicably look into the minds of humans. Why he was getting a vague, spotter's eye impression of the entire baseball field. What Charles had been doing on his phone while Reginald had been talking to Walker. Why, beyond mere visual similarity, he'd thought how much vampire and human troops looked alike in uniform. Reginald's mental abilities were sticky; sometimes he had to be staring directly at an issue and asking exactly the right questions in order to see the obvious. But now that Claude had spoken, his mind asked the questions and got all the answers. He sent his mind out to the crowd of humans, recognizing the now-obvious fact that they weren't all humans. His blood found Charles, Walker, and at least two dozen of the most elite, former V-Crew troops the USVC (and formerly the Annihilist Faction) had to offer.

Lafontaine turned, not understanding why the big guard had spoken. Reginald tried to warn him, but Claude had the human in a body lock in less than the blink of an eye, his big arm cocked around Lafontaine's neck. Claude was dressed head-to-toe in armor, including gloves and boots. As he moved, Reginald could see that his gloves were doubled and that every seam and crack and crevice in the armor had been sealed. Claude held Lafontaine for ten, fifteen seconds without reacting in pain, without indicating that the humans' weapon had sneaked past his defenses.

Claude's movement happened so fast that the humans, who'd been looking outward rather than among their own for threats, didn't react. By the time they caught a sense of what might be happening and began to stir, the other vampires in human armor had moved to strike, each subduing one or two humans each. The entire thing happened so quickly that it seemed rehearsed. It almost certainly had been. The movements were precise and practiced — the actions of seasoned experts. The exchange took two beats. One-two, and the balance of power had flipped.

Keeping Lafontaine restrained, Claude used his free hand to remove his own helmet.

"Hot as hell in there," he said. "You'd think they'd make this shit more comfortable, seeing as they're warm-blooded."

Two of the soldiers walked forward. When they were halfway to the pitcher's mound, one of the two pushed the other back, placing a hand on his chest. The snubbed soldier made a pouty little motion with his body and Reginald immediately realized that it was Charles. Which would make the other...

"Walker," said Reginald. Then he added, "You titanic piece of shit."

Walker removed his helmet and stood beside Claude.

He whispered something into the big vampire's ear, and Claude nodded. Walker waved Charles forward. Charles removed his own helmet and then, taking a cue, several of the undercover vampires around the field removed theirs. They'd executed the maneuver flawlessly. Every single human had been covered and neutralized, already disarmed and laying in the dirt with their hands behind them. Not a single shot had been fired, and not a single punch had been thrown.

Nikki, still bound, spit at Walker. A blob of white saliva landed on his cheek. He wiped it away and smiled a smile that was the exact opposite of his normal one.

"Hey," he said, "it's like this guy said." Walker pointed at Lafontaine. "We're between a rock and a hard place. What did you expect me to do? What did you think was going to happen to us if he found out that I'd helped you, which he absolutely would have?"

"You could have just *not* helped us," said Reginald, feeling genuine anger boil inside himself. He began reaching out — not just with tendrils of thought, but with fists. He wanted to claw his way inside Claude's and Walker's and Charles's minds, then do some damage. But Charles seemed to feel that they'd done the right thing in alerting the president to treachery, and both Walker and Claude had raised solid mental barriers against Reginald's intrusion. His only hope was finding a way to distract them. Keeping Reginald out seemed to require constant effort. With their attention focused on his intrusion, maybe they'd miss something else.

Like Nikki, who was bound in silver.

Or Reginald, who was weak and slow.

And that was it. Just the two of them. There was no other help to be had.

The humans were all down, all literally under the gun. Claude had thought of everything.

"They have bombs, Reggie," said Walker. "Big bombs filled with black tar."

"It's actually an antivirus," said Lafontaine. Claude raised a boot and kicked him in the head.

Walker continued: "Once we picked off a few of their troops on the way here, we found one of their walkies with the security code still entered while we were putting on their armor. There's a bomb in New York and one in Geneva, but they were talking like there are a bunch more. We don't know where they are, but we know they're there. And after you got done with your little chat, he was going to kill us all."

"Still can," Lafontaine croaked. Claude kicked him again.

"We'll find them," he said, glancing at the human. "Especially if you can't phone home and tell them that we spoiled your party."

"The bombs are set off *unless* the others hear from us," said Lafontaine, smiling around a mouthful of bloody teeth. "Is this your first tangle with someone willing to use a dead man's switch?"

Claude shook his head. "We'll find them," he repeated.

Lafontaine spat blood into the dirt. "This doesn't matter. Kill everyone here or let us live. Either way, we win."

But they didn't win. *Nobody* won. Reginald felt his panic return, now exacerbated by the presence of yet more people who wanted to kill first and listen to what Reginald had to say later. Claude and the others had signed their own death warrants. Even if they found every single bomb, what would come next? They couldn't exterminate humanity, and they wouldn't be able to subdue them this time. The edge of that particular knife had become too sharp. At this point, the remaining humans would rather die than bleed.

"You assholes," said Reginald. "I came here for a reason. None of you have any idea what you're messing with."

"They can't kill us all," said Claude.

"Oh yes we can," said Lafontaine.

Claude looked down. His eyes flashed. He used his fist to strike the man very hard, suddenly incautious about whatever infection he may have slathered on his skin. Lafontaine's head reeled, his movements conveying a swimminess that his lack of eyes couldn't. He didn't reply. He was lucky that the punch hadn't killed him.

Claude picked Lafontaine up by the collar, lifting him off the ground, and bellowed into his face.

"YOU ARE NOT IN CHARGE! THIS IS NOT YOUR WORLD! THIS IS OUR WORLD!"

Lafontaine smiled slightly and mumbled, "The meek shall inherit the Earth."

Claude dropped him, leaving the man to sputter in the baseball diamond's dust and chalk. A bloody spit bubble came out of his mouth and popped, leaving a ring of red residue. Claude, above him, put his hands on his hips, looking around. The other vampires watched Claude. Then Claude turned and kicked Lafontaine in the ribs, making his body jump. He stooped down, again yelling in the resistance leader's ear.

"WE ARE ON TOP! YOU ARE FOOD! JUST MOTHERFUCKING FOOD, DO YOU HEAR ME?"

Reginald looked over the top of Claude's head. Walker was watching Claude. Charles was watching Walker.

"This is your president," said Reginald.

Claude's head snapped up. His wide eyes met Reginald's, and his tirade turned from the human to the fat vampire in chains.

"DON'T YOU MOTHERFUCKING MOUTH OFF! YOU WITH YOUR FUCKING HUMAN-LOVING, COMPASSIONATE BULLSHIT!"

Reginald looked Claude in the eye. He kept his voice calm, pitching it so the others could hear. "Compassion isn't only for humans. The problem with you is that you've never had any loyalty. Not to your president. Not to your so-called friends and allies. Not even to your own brother."

"IT'S FOR THE WEAK!"

"Calm down," said Reginald. He tried to get inside, tried to get behind Claude's eyes. He'd glamoured him before, but that had been before Claude had known who Reginald was or what he could do. Reginald's lips asked Claude to calm down. His eyes asked Claude to calm down. But beyond that, he had no influence, and Claude wasn't listening. But it hardly mattered. None of what he was saying was for Claude's ears. It was for the others.

Reginald met Nikki's eye. She was behind Claude, in front of Walker, still standing. Claude's leash on her had loosened, but she would never be able to outmuscle him. Reginald considered going into her head, trying to use her like a puppet, but there was nothing he could use. Claude had no weapons Nikki could grab; the human soldiers didn't carry sidearms and Claude had left his rifle behind when he'd brought her out. She'd have to use her hands, and even if those hands could outmatch a vampire two millennia her senior (which they couldn't), she was weak from the silver. Besides, Walker was still behind her. Her hands, behind her back, were directly in front of him, and he'd see her move before Claude did. And of course, there was still Charles to think about.

"You think you're better than us," Claude said, his eyes boring into Reginald's soul. "You always have. I know all about you, you know. I know what you can do with your mind. I know how you escaped from the Council, by sticking your hand inside the heads of the others. I know how you and Maurice were always trying to…"

"Don't you *dare* mention Maurice," said Reginald.

"… to enact some meatbag-loving law or another, to create all these inferior, fat, ugly, damaged fucking poor-excuse-for-a-vampire vampires. I know how you tried to save all those condemned wanton creation criminals, like yourself. And I know how, while we were trying to clear the planet of these *pests*, you were working to save them. Even when you came to Antarctica, you were fighting against us, and that's why we followed you: because we knew what kind of a pathetic, weak-willed piece of shit you were. And so yes, I killed Timken. Because he was weak, like you. He took the ball most of the way, but as I'd always known he would, he fell short at the very end."

Claude was bent at the waist, his breath hot on Reginald's face as his final mask of civility dropped away and his true face emerged. His eyes seemed to burn. Saliva pooled in his mouth and his fangs descended. A line of spit fell from his lower lip as he spoke, unheeded.

"Timken got soft," he said. "He *wanted* to talk to the humans when they reached out. He wanted to *negotiate*. He was even considering *letting them go!* As a gesture of goodwill. And that's how he said it, too: 'A gesture of goodwill.' As if we had to pacify these animals. As if they weren't ours to use in whatever way we saw fit. I wanted to tighten human movement within the farms and harvest more from the wildlands to join them, to shake up the gene pool. But Timken? He once proposed giving them a protected furlough once a year. And somehow, he expected them to come back without a fight? He expected the taste of freedom to not incite riots? Can you imagine it?"

"Compassion," said Reginald, nodding slightly. "Believe it or not, I can imagine it just fine."

Claude straightened. He didn't look precisely angry, and that in itself was frightening. It was as if he'd gone beyond anger, as if he'd rolled right into a place where anger was pointless because it was impossible for anyone to disagree.

He turned and grabbed Nikki's chain. He didn't grab one of the loose ends. Instead, he grabbed the circle around her neck, the backs of his gloved knuckles against her throat. Then he dragged her closer, holding her at his side in front of Reginald.

"I know about *her*, too," Claude said, turning his gaze toward Nikki. He regarded her for a second, seeming to scent her, his mouth open just far enough for his fangs to show. "Nicole Pilson. She was approved by Council before you got your hands on her. I looked up her evaluation, you know. Prime scores. Excellent strength, agility, and cunning. An appropriately dark backstory. Oh, she was *made* to be a vampire. Except for one thing: her *compassion*, as you say. She had her whole eternity ahead of her, but then she met you and it all fell apart. Impersonating a vampire. Treason. Murder. She backed Maurice, went rogue. All because she had *compassion* for the poor man who didn't measure up. Because of that, she threw it all away."

"She's a vampire now, Claude," said Reginald. His undead heart was starting to accelerate. He remembered how Maurice had come to his rescue and prayed for strength, but none came. So this would be his final failure: his progeny was in mortal peril, and the vampire agent in his blood wouldn't even rise to help him.

Claude looked at Reginald, then back at Nikki. Now his mouth opened further, his fangs very near Nikki's long, smooth neck. Reginald watched her swallow as Walker looked on from behind them.

"She *is* a vampire now, isn't she?" he said. "Oh yes. Thanks to an act of wanton creation, because she wanted to be with you — and you, knowing you shouldn't, had *compassion* enough to turn her anyway. The lines are fuzzy, following your criminal overthrow, but that's how I'd judge her. And even if her creation wasn't wanton, it was tainted. Because *you* were her maker. You, who should never have been here in the first place. You, who should have been left to die — but weren't, because Maurice had *compassion* for you."

He looked at Reginald, then at Nikki, and then back at Reginald. He shook his head in a way that was almost sad. His eyes were somewhere else, departed from sanity. Saliva dripped from his fangs, then ran down his chin. His fist, holding tight to Nikki's neck chain, was shaking. He was gripping it so hard that Reginald found himself hoping that the gloves would split against the silver, burning him.

"So many mistakes," he said. "So many bleeding hearts. No vampire should exist because of pity, because it is our *ruthlessness* that makes us strong. Lafontaine never should have met you tonight. If he'd blown his bombs out of hand, we'd be on our way to extinct. I won't make that same mistake. A vampire should never hesitate. When faced with an enemy, he should kill it. Not *love* it. Not *forgive* it." As he concluded, his nose brushed Nikki's chin just above the chain. His fangs grazed her skin. Reginald saw her flinch.

"Please," said Reginald, his voice breaking.

"*Please* is for the weak," said Claude. "*Pity* is for the weak. *Mercy*, Reginald, is for the weak. We are strong. As your human friends are about to learn, all *mercy* will get you is a knife in the back."

"Or a silver-lined meat fork pulled from your shoulder," said a voice.

Claude turned, but not fast enough. Todd Walker had been born to be a vampire. He'd been strong and fast even on his first night, when Nikki had begged Maurice not to kill him after Maurice had impaled him with that fork. Walker's gloved hands flipped the chain from Nikki's neck to Claude's in milliseconds. But it didn't last for long; Walker, who'd survived through Nikki's mercy, immediately began to falter. Claude was two thousand years old, and stronger in spite of the silver.

Reginald met Nikki's eye.

"Get him," he said.

Nikki, now free and unencumbered, struck at Claude with an outstretched hand, her fingers pressed together and straight. Her nails speared him through the neck, emerging at the back. Her other hand joined the first and she pulled, and a moment later Maurice's killer's head struck the dirt. Then Walker and Nikki stepped back as Claude's body began to spark and burn, and in seconds he was nothing but ash.

Charles turned and ran.

The vampire soldiers around the field began to buckle and twitch as Reginald, still chained to the folding metal chair, reached into their minds. Vampire adrenaline came in the form of a late-stage cavalry, finally flooding his system as he watched Claude burn. He felt his blood's intelligence grow fists. He saw the mental walls the soldiers had raised and blasted effortlessly through them. Then he had the vampires by their throats, all of them at the ends of arms of thought, all with their rotted brains clenched in his grip, squeezing and churning.

Guns turned on their holders. They were re-appropriated human weapons, so when the vampires around the field began to fire on themselves, black blooms formed around the gunshots and they began to light up the night with their screams. Reginald reached inside one of the soldiers and, feeling anger like a torch, made him pull the pin on the UV grenade strapped to the belt he'd stolen. The grenade exploded, setting him on fire.

Then the vampires ran. There was no nobility, no loyalty, no thought given to loathed human compassion. Those who could still run became streaks in the night. Reginald felt them go, watching their thoughts and emotions diminish into the night.

When the vampires were gone, the humans rose to their feet and re-claimed their dropped weapons. Then, one by one, they began to train them on the three vampires still left in the middle of the field.

Reginald looked down at Lafontaine. The big man was bloody but alive.

"It's over," said Reginald.

Lafontaine spat blood, climbing onto his knees. "It's not over."

Around the field, guns flashed red dots. Reginald watched as Nikki and Walker's chests were painted with them, skittering across their fronts like fireflies. He looked down. The dots were on him too. He was still bound, still unable to flee even if he'd wanted to. Nikki and Walker couldn't even carry him, thanks to all the silver.

Reginald met Lafontaine's sightless eyes, knowing that the man could see him. "I saved you," he said.

The red spots clustered tighter. Human soldiers took to their knees, steading their aim.

"You *betrayed* me."

"I wasn't behind what just happened. They betrayed me, too."

Lafontaine stood. Once he was up, he was steady. He looked strong, even. Determined. "Your kind is always 'behind it,' and that's the problem," he said.

"We need to talk. I came here to talk." He felt the mood on the field, realizing that what he'd thought earlier was still true: he was able to feel the emotions of the humans even though he was sure that all of the vampires were gone. The mood he felt wasn't good, or trusting, or even compassionate enough to give him the slightest benefit of the doubt.

His voice dropped to pleading, making him hate himself as he heard it but knowing that time was running out. "We *have* to talk."

Lafontaine pulled a walkie from his belt. He keyed in a code.

"What are you doing?" said Nikki.

"Ending New York," he said. "Ending Geneva."

"We just saved you! Look at what just happened here!" Nikki begged.

Lafontaine shook his head. "There's no other way. We will never be safe as long as you continue to live."

"Please," said Reginald. "Give me five minutes."

"Vampirekind has already had too many minutes."

"We have to talk! All you have to do is listen!"

Lafontaine's empty eye sockets met Reginald's. He shook his head, and said, "I don't want to listen."

Then Reginald saw it.

Inside his mind — inside his *blood* — Reginald saw a vision of 28 opening doors. He saw the doors circling a rotunda at the end of a corridor, and he could feel the corridor as much as he could feel the doors. He knew what was coming. He knew what had changed. He saw the missing piece — the piece of the codex that finally cleared away the fog of indecision. And he knew what he had to do.

Around the baseball field, in exact synchronicity, all 28 of the human soldiers turned their guns around as the vampires had, pressing the muzzles to the undersides of their chins.

Lafontaine watched his troops turn their guns on themselves, their movements as perfectly coordinated as a water ballet. Then he lowered the walkie, his mouth hanging open.

"Now will you listen?" said Reginald.

EIGHTEEN

Listen

Claire walked onto the baseball field like a lion tamer entering a circle of animals she's subdued. There was a second folding metal chair near the dugout. She picked it up and dragged it to the pitcher's mound, set it across from Reginald and Lafontaine, then reached toward the human and plucked the walkie from his unprotesting hand. She gave the walkie to Nikki, who pocketed it, then sat on the chair backward, her chest against the backrest.

"All my life," she said, addressing Lafontaine, "I knew I was different. At first I just didn't fit in, and I thought it was just because I was a strange kid — smaller, picked on, smarter than most and with a strange knack for getting my mom and other adults to let me do what I wanted. I was good with computers. I once outran a bunch of bullies who had much longer legs than mine, and I outran Reginald when I first met him."

"To be fair," said Reginald, "I was also outrun by several other people that week."

Claire smiled at him — her too-young face suddenly making sense. Then she looked at his chains, and he felt something in them shift and change, and then the links broke and they fell to the dirt.

"But when I got older and I realized that my father was an incubus, I started to develop new skills that were beyond 'strange.' I got good at moving energy around. I became a hacker who didn't need to hack. And I got all this *noise* in my head. And then I got sick for a while, and I really remember that because, looking back, I never got sick before then. Literally *never*. I had never had a cold, the flu, a stomach ache, an infection… not even a cut that lasted for long. I looked into it later — after the war, after I found my skin growing cold and realized I could pass for vampire. I decided that I had exceptional mind-body control, like a yogi. So I tried to manipulate myself consciously and found that I could slow my heartbeat, warm my skin if I wanted. All sorts of things. I looked back on that sickness, more curious than ever, and realized that it had happened right after all of my other abilities had started to show and right before my aging slowed down." She put her hand beside her mouth and whispered at Lafontaine as if she were conveying a secret. "I'm 51! But don't tell anyone, okay?"

Lafontaine looked from Reginald to Nikki to Claire. He even looked up at Walker, who seemed dumbfounded. Then he looked around the field, at the humans still holding guns to their throats.

Reginald met Claire's eyes. Inside, with a connection they'd never shared before, he asked her if it would be safe to let the humans go. Her mind told his that the men with guns wouldn't — and, in her presence, *couldn't* — hurt them now. So Reginald dropped his mass-glamour: a new kind of glamour that reached up from inside, through the blood, like walking the vampire family tree — now available for humans, too. The soldiers lowered their weapons, then turned to watch the events unfolding in the field's middle.

Claire opened her mouth and licked her upper row of teeth. Two of them descended into fangs. Reginald looked at Nikki, who said nothing.

"Now, today," Claire continued, "I realize that I was always kind of a vampire. But I was something else, too. I could walk in the sunlight. I wasn't as fast or as strong as true vampires. Even though I aged slowly, I did age. Right up until the moment Nikki turned me, just tonight, it never really made sense. But now I see it. I see how the potential to become a vampire — a *half* vampire, anyway — was always there. It was always inside of me." She turned to Lafontaine. "The same as it's inside of you," she added.

Lafontaine, seemingly unwilling to trust his feet, sat on the dirt of the mound. "What do you mean?"

"I have the ability to manipulate energy. At first, it was just a neat trick. Reginald said I could tell the future. But of course I couldn't tell the future. I made it up. I told the angels — do you know about the vampire angels? — that I knew a war was coming and that Reginald would lead a great change in the vampires of the world. The angels wanted to kill them all. But I think we showed them another way things could unfold, though we got lucky in that they couldn't tell I was bluffing. But the thing is, I *wasn't* bluffing; I just didn't know it. Soon after I realized I could make computers do things. Anything electronic. I could push signals anywhere I wanted. I could float into the most secure computers. My hands would make this neat blue lightning. But what I realized, once I put two and two together with the way I could change my body as I needed, was that I had been healing myself all along. It was mind over matter, very literally. I was surrounded by vampires. I always wanted to be one. So my body *made* me one — or at least, half of one."

"How?" said Lafontaine.

Reginald stepped in, putting what Lafontaine had told him together with what he'd just learned from the codex's final piece. "It's not just a virus," he said. "It's a *retro*virus."

"V? You mean it's…?"

Reginald nodded. "It's part of you, yes. In vampires, it makes us what we are. But in humans, it's dormant. Unless, of course —" He gestured to Claire. "— you can manipulate your own body through force of will."

"Or desire," Claire added. She resituated herself on the chair, crossing her arms over the backrest. "What I've realized about vampire blood, now that my veins are full of it, is that it's conscious. It's not just a bunch of machinery. It holds memories and desires, and all of those things are passed from maker to progeny. That's why Reginald can access it within himself, and how he was able to put together an ancient puzzle. But for me, I didn't realize that I'd woken up those genes before being turned. I just knew that I was manifesting vampire traits. I got cold. I aged slowly. I was somewhat faster than normal, somewhat stronger than normal. I didn't get sick, and when I got cut, it healed quickly. It was my ability to change my body combining with the awakening consciousness of my vampire blood."

Nikki squatted beside her, and Reginald was touched to see how motherly the gesture was. Nikki had been on the planet for 79 years to Claire's 51, but right now they looked the same age. They'd outgrown their mother-daughter appearance in the past years, but the bond had never left Nikki's heart.

"How did you have vampire blood?" she asked. "Were you bitten?"

"My mother had it," she said.

"Was she bitten before the time that almost killed her?"

"No. Her mother and father had it."

Nikki looked at Reginald.

"This is what I found when I completed the codex," said Reginald, looking alternately at Nikki and Lafontaine. "The virus is copied into the DNA of human hosts when they're bitten. It's like how a mosquito sort of backwashes into you when it bites you, and why infected mosquitos can spread diseases like West Nile and malaria. You don't turn, but the virus is still there, and it's copied down the line, from parent to child."

"Do you mean that every...?" Lafontaine began.

"Every human has it, yes," said Reginald. "Vampires have been around long enough for it to filter into all of you."

"So what does that mean?"

Reginald shrugged. "It means that you need us and we need you."

"You need us," said Lafontaine. "We merely *have* you."

"No," said Reginald, shaking his head. "You *need* us. You've heard about the humans raised in blood farms getting sick?"

"Yes. We assumed it was the kind of minor plague that festers in contained groups. We were going to test the humans when they were released, but..." He didn't have to finish the sentence: ... *but your president had them all killed.*

Reginald nodded, sighing. Then he said, "But think about it. If it were something being spread around in a contained population, why would it be present in *all* of the contained populations? Because in case your people haven't done the research, I'll just tell you: *every* blood farm is reporting sickness and losses."

"So what is it?"

Claire looked at the human. "Forty years of the kids not coming home," she said.

"Farm humans aren't fed on," said Reginald. "They're drained with machinery. It's ludicrous: a bunch of undead monsters, while they were building TVs and making infomercials for blood pills and learning to like human junk food, became germophobes. There are only a few ways to kill vampires, and normal germs aren't one of them. But even so, the blood farms had very, very strict rules that prohibited guards and employees from feeding on the stock. So in all that time — two generations — those populations didn't get fresh infusions of what you call the V virus. It's unstable over time, and if an interbreeding population isn't fed on, it begins to fall apart."

"Are you saying that without vampires, we'd..."

"You'd die," said Reginald.

Lafontaine looked at Nikki's pocket, where his walkie was stowed. Reginald, thanks to the bridge Claire's hybrid blood had made between the species, could feel his fear — his sense of a crisis barely averted. He could feel something else coming from the human, too: blessedly, Lafontaine believed what he was hearing. He sat back on the packed dirt of the pitcher's mound, his hands propping him up, his elbows straight. He looked weak.

"So we're stuck," he said. "There's no way to win."

"There's something else," said Reginald. "Something that may make you feel less stuck."

Lafontaine looked up, again acting oddly like a sighted man. But then again, Reginald thought, human sonar wasn't something he knew much about. Maybe the man had to look where he wanted to "see" so that his ears could help his brain form pictures.

"Did you ever wonder why you were able to so easily outmatch us this time?" he said.

Lafontaine shrugged, asking Reginald to continue.

"In the vampire population, the virus runs the body. It's like an engine. But when it's not working to make systems work — when it's latent, and is just being replicated as new cells are made, which is what happens in humans — it spins off a bit of debris that does, in a small way, give you a touch of vampire blood."

"*Intelligent* blood," Claire added. "*Conscious* blood."

"You don't know it's happening, but the consciousness in the blood talks to your human brain."

"I'd say *spirit,*" said Claire, looking thoughtful.

"Spirit. Sure, I guess. Consciousness is something that rises above individual thoughts — an 'emergent property', they call it. And that's what that touch of vampire blood... let's say '*communes*' with. Consciousness and creativity and intelligence are technically in the brain... but it's almost more accurate to say they're '*out there*' somehow as well."

Lafontaine said something that Reginald didn't catch. Reginald was thinking of Maurice, his memories, and his presence in Reginald's blood, speaking with what Reginald had assumed was Reginald's own authority.

"Sorry?"

"I said, 'So what does that mean?'"

"It means that while vampire brains stagnate with our bodies — enhanced, yes, but forever locked in that enhanced state, save small changes over very long periods of time — the same blood inside humans causes *your* brains to grow."

"*Spirits,*" Claire corrected.

"It makes you intelligent, in other words. That bit of vampire blood *gives* you emergent properties, like intelligence and self-awareness. And curiosity."

"I said earlier that I'd never seen a curious vampire," said Lafontaine. "Until you."

Reginald shrugged. That was one mystery he didn't know the answer to. But then again, most vampires couldn't do most of the things Reginald could do. Maybe he was a kind of biological version of the codex — something that had, after millennia of trial and error, finally combined into a perfect configuration. He couldn't help himself; he looked down at his body as he thought it. The idea of Reginald Baskin as the universe's perfect being was delightfully ridiculous. He thought again of Maurice, saying, *You are what you are. Fatass.*

"Without vampires," Reginald continued, "the blood farm populations were getting sick and stupid. And without humans to copy and steal from, even our ability to feed off of you wasn't enough to save us. Each species needs the other. We're a perfect symbiosis."

"Like a tapeworm," said Claire.

"Claire," said Reginald, "that's a parasite."

"*Sooo-ry,*" she droned, waving her hands. "Someone destroyed the world before I got to high school."

NINETEEN

Slapfight

Lafontaine believed. It was enough.

They retired to a human stronghold away from the open air of the baseball field an hour before sunrise. The vampire troops, seemingly frightened to their cores by Reginald's ability to seize them by their brainstems, didn't return. The humans loaded into the vehicles they'd arrived in, and Lafontaine, who suspected his men might not be convinced of the interlopers' good intent (especially after they'd been forced to point their guns at their own heads) kept the vampires separate, giving them their own truck. Walker declined to go with them and refused all thanks and praise. Nikki told him that he'd been noble. Walker told her that her tits looked fantastic. Then he was gone, like an asshole in the night.

Brian, Nikki reported, had run "somewhere safe" after she'd turned Claire. He wasn't specific about where he was going, but Brian was a big boy and could handle himself, and Reginald's blood would lead them to him when the time came. So they rode as a troika, almost afraid to speak and break what felt like a delicate spell. They didn't *need* to speak, though; Reginald accepted the flow of thoughts that Claire, who'd joined the vampire family tree and was now accessible through Nikki, offered him. Her mental images came in a burst, but he slowed his processing to see all of their colors: Claire meditating to calm herself after Reginald had left, her realization about herself and the virus, and her request to Nikki. Reginald nodded at Claire as he finished the mental tour, telling her that he understood. She'd made a bridge between the conscious blood of vampires and the latent intelligence inherent in human blood. The two species were more alike than they were different — despite all of the hunting, the fangs, and their differing mortality.

"This still doesn't solve anything, you know," said Nikki.

Reginald looked over. "How so?"

"Vampires still need to feed on humans, and the humans aren't going to want them to."

"Vampires can be made to understand," said Reginald. "Once they know what's at stake."

"What *is* at stake?" said Nikki.

"He's talking about the angels," said Claire from the back seat. "I told you that, Nikki."

She looked back. "When?"

"When I asked you to turn me. When I realized the truth about the fog."

In Reginald's mind, he watched the image Claire sent him: a thick white cloud, parting in a breeze. Claire's knowledge of the future had faltered when she'd reached the fog, and Reginald's had faltered when he'd completed the codex and had seen, in a similar fog, that the predestined timeline had reached its end. The codex spoke about a human uprising, but not about whether the uprising would mean the end of everything. It was like seeing a gunshot but not where the bullet struck.

The fog had meant that a decision had to be made before the future could roll forward. And as soon as Claire had realized that the decision was her own decision to become a vampire, everything had cleared.

"I don't remember," said Nikki.

"That's because you have a dumb vampire brain," said Claire.

Nikki reached into the backseat and slapped playfully at Claire. It had the feel of a mother acting silly with her daughter, but to anyone on the outside it would look like a slapfight between sisters.

When they were done sparring, Claire said, "The angels talked about evolution. Charles and Timken and Claude and the others took that to mean they had to evolve into the dominant species on the planet — to 'win the game' against humans, due to that dumb Cain and Abel myth."

"So there was no Cain and Abel?"

"There was a Cain," said Reginald. "I don't know about Abel. But when I went all the way back, I didn't see fighting, or a contest, or a bet, or any of the things the myth talks about."

"Reginald, on the other hand," Claire continued, "interpreted 'evolution' to mean becoming more human. What was it the angels told you, Reginald?"

"'They became whole. You remained half,'" he quoted.

"But what I think that actually meant was *the blood itself* needed to change. Humans and vampires were 'half' of each other. And while humans embraced the creativity and innovation given to them by the vampire virus, vampires took nothing back from humans. Other than food, that is."

"So what are they supposed to take back?"

203

"An evolved virus, maybe," said Claire.

"And how does that happen?"

"Nikki! Didn't you listen to anything I told you? Did you just think I wanted to become a vampire so I'd have some cool pointy teeth?"

"Hey," said Nikki, pointing a red-fingernailed finger sternly back at Claire, "don't make me slap you again."

"In the codex," said Reginald, "the one thing I couldn't make sense of until tonight was the mention it made of a missing link that would come from the unresolved conflict."

Nikki looked at him, not getting it. So Reginald, keeping his eyes on the road, flopped a lazy finger back at Claire.

Nikki craned over the seat. "You're the missing link?"

"Apparently," said Claire.

"Like a caveman?"

"You're the one with the dumb brain," said Claire. Nikki tried again to slap her, but Claire pivoted away and retaliated with a bag of Cheetos that was lying on the backseat. *Real* Cheetos, not clones, which meant that they'd been around for at least forty years. Old Reginald would have eaten them anyway, convinced that something so artificial would be perfect for a vampire, seeing as it never aged.

"How are *you* the missing link?"

Claire shifted in the back seat. "Shut up."

"I'm serious," said Nikki. And then, out of the corner of his eye, Reginald watched as Nikki put on an overly serious face. It looked ludicrous.

"When I took your blood," Claire explained, "I changed it. I could see it as if it were in front of my eyes. I moved the blocks around and made it into something new. I 'made it my own' as they used to say on certain dearly departed reality singing shows."

"So what is it now?"

Claire thought for a moment. "Something new," she said.

"So you're not like us?"

"Not in any way you'll notice," said Claire. Then, in the rearview mirror, Reginald watched her eyes dart around mischievously and she added, "Except that I'll be smarter than your dumb vampire brain."

Nikki tried to hit her again.

"She's right, though," said Reginald. Nikki moved to hit him and the car swerved, causing their human escort, speared in the headlights ahead, to hit the brakes in alarm. Nikki lowered her arm and Reginald, begging for mercy, continued. "If the codex's implications are right, she'll heal the gap. She'll allow for a slightly different exchange between the species, based on a modified vampire phenotype. *Very* slightly different. It'll take generations to filter down through everyone, if not centuries or even millennia as the humans repopulate."

"What's a a phenotype?" said Claire.

"It's the way the germ shows up in the body, dumbass," said Nikki. Then she turned and whispered to Reginald, *"I figured it out from context."*

"But *that* will help the vampires to understand, too," said Reginald. "Over time, they'll get used to the idea that humans aren't just food, but are actually the opposite halves of themselves. Like night and day."

"And the humans?" said Nikki. "You expect them to just lay down their arms, bare their necks, and make friends?"

"In a way," said Reginald. "But more accurately, I expect them to forget."

"Oh, right," said Nikki. *"That's* logical." But when she looked over at Reginald, she saw that he was tapping his head, indicating his own vampire brain — the one that got smarter rather than dumber, that was like a codex in itself. A brain that was more than the sum of its parts, featuring millions of collections of vampire memories housed forever in conscious, emergent blood.

"Just like that, huh?" said Nikki.

"Just like that."

"Can you do it now?"

"I could, yes. But Lafontaine needs to remember. Others will need to remember, too. There will always need to be some humans who know all of what happened. To be shepherds of the secret — to oversee the birth of a new codex."

There was a snapping motion from the back seat, and Reginald looked into the rear view mirror to see that Claire had discovered an ancient Coca-Cola to go with the Cheetos and had just cracked it open. She was drinking it, taking it in in long swallows.

"Gross, Claire," said Reginald. "That Coke is at least forty years old."

Claire shrugged. "Hey, what else am I supposed to drink? Blood?"

TWENTY

Sunrise

Reginald sat on the front porch, looking east, watching the barest blush of red begin to creep onto the horizon. To a lot of vampires, it might look like a suicide in progress, but he'd gotten this down to a science. When the first true yellow began to appear, he'd start to feel warm. The front door was literally right behind him, and he'd duck inside. Even if some joker with a deadly sense of humor locked the door, he could run around the side and dive through a window. It was glass, and they'd never installed steel shutters. But he liked this dangerous little game. He liked to feel the warmth on his skin, to feel as alive as a dead man could feel.

"Mind if I sit with you?" said a voice.

Reginald looked up at the tall man standing on the deck behind him.

"Oh, Jesus," he moaned.

"Not quite," said the man. He stooped down and sat beside Reginald, looking eastward. He appeared to be in his seventies and had a narrow, hawklike face. He also had piercing blue eyes that, Reginald knew from experience, could look at the forthcoming sun without harm.

"Do you want some blood?" said Reginald, raising a pouch. They'd need to start hunting again soon, and Reginald, with his four decades of slightly improved speed, might even be able to catch a victim. Still, he'd miss the farmed blood. It had been so convenient, like his old life of fast food and television had been. But he hadn't been fat anywhere but on his fleshy body for a long time, and while he'd miss the convenience of packaged blood, he wouldn't really, deep down, be sad to see it go.

"I don't drink blood," said the man.

"How about a Coke?"

"Real Coke, or that shit your company started making when all the humans died?"

Reginald turned and met the man's gaze. It wasn't as threatening of a gaze as it had once been. "You saw that?" he said.

The old man shrugged. "I'm an angel. We're supposed to watch over you."

"But you're an *evil* angel."

Balestro raised his wrinkled hand, held it level, then wiggled it to indicate that hairs were being split. "Meh."

"It's real Coke," said Reginald. "Claire found a six-pack in the back seat of a human car. It kept surprisingly well. I had one for nostalgic reasons."

Balestro kept looking into the distance, nodding. "Yeah, bring me one."

When Reginald returned with the drink, the angel was still sitting where Reginald had left him. Some part of him had been convinced that he'd been an apparition and would be gone, but he was still there, still as corporeal as ever, still looking exactly as he had all those years ago on the hilltop in Germany when he'd surrounded them with the fabled Ring of Fire. Reginald could see it in his mind as clearly as if it were yesterday.

"We couldn't have done it, you know," said Balestro, not looking up until Reginald nudged him with the can of Coke. Then he did look up, smiled a thank you, and took the red can from Reginald's hand. Reginald could have put it in a glass with ice, but this was an angel. Angels were certainly badass enough to drink from cans, and would laugh at Earthly niceties such as ice.

"You couldn't have done what?" said Reginald.

"Killed you all with the Ring of Fire."

Reginald looked over at Balestro's hawklike profile. Then he looked back toward the blush on the horizon, which had brightened.

"I figured as much."

"Your deaths or your survival had to come from your own decisions," he said. "We can't kill anyone. We have to find a way to get you to decide to walk willingly into demise, or fight to live."

Reginald nodded. Maurice had told him the same thing years ago. At the time, the fact that angels couldn't circumvent free will had seemed to be just one more datum in a game filled with arbitrary rules and rituals. *Can't enter a human's house. Piercing of the heart by wood — but not by anything else — will kill a vampire. Can't glamour humans into letting you into their homes, or into submitting to slavery.* It was all so random. But once Reginald had solved the codex, the ritualistic nature of Heavenly decrees had stuck out like a loose thread in a tapestry, and he'd begun to wonder if that big pyrotechnic display had all been for show — a way to push vampires toward conflict so that they could be made to die fighting.

"Dirty trick," said Reginald, sipping his pouch of blood.

"It was nothing personal. We did it for your own good."

"Hey," said Reginald. "All's well that ends well. The way I see it, seven billion people died horrible deaths due to a fear of something that never existed. And also, we were almost consumed by a biological weapon in dirty bombs, which would have killed both species." Reginald raised his blood pouch, touched it to the side of Balestro's soda can in a toast. "It's all good."

After a moment, the angel said, "You were dead anyway."

Reginald turned.

"If we could have exterminated you, we would have, to clear this planet and start over. Spurring you to war was almost as good, seeing as whatever you did in a war would only harden your enemies — who you knew you couldn't eliminate no matter what — to fight better against you. When you were turned, Reginald, you saw how vampires used to be. They were arrogant and growing stupider by the year. They were asking for extinction."

"And that justified all those deaths? To stop vampires from being arrogant and fancy and sparkly? To stop Charles's fashion victim wardrobe and perfect hair?"

The angel turned to face Reginald. His gaze was like an X-ray, and Reginald felt more naked than naked. He felt transparent, as if his metaphysical fly was open and his soul was flapping in the breeze.

"Like I said, you were dead anyway."

Reginald felt himself becoming angry. "What the hell does that mean?"

"You'd broken the natural cycle. You were bottle-necked. You'd stopped evolving."

"Is this about Claire?"

The angel laughed. "Claire. The incubus's daughter."

He laughed again, and the sound rattled Reginald's bones. He hadn't seen Balestro smile before; he hadn't even thought it was possible. "When you live forever and have access to the dominoes of fate, it certainly is nice to be surprised."

"So it's *not* about Claire."

"She was a pleasant surprise. And proof that not even Heaven knows everything. You're building an unknown future right now. Even we don't know what will happen next." He turned to look at Reginald. "Yet, anyway."

Reginald didn't know if the angel was being honest or just screwing with him. Based on what Claire had told him, seeing the future was merely a matter of knowing everything in the universe. Not a terribly big task for an angel, really.

"No, it's not about her," Balestro continued. "We may have deceived you about the Ring of Fire, but we told you the truth about the bottleneck. Humans evolved but you did not. Vampires aren't curious like humans are. They stick in one place. And that was mostly okay, because it was how you were and it couldn't be helped. But then you started to extend those prejudices into your society. You only turned people of a certain type, and the vampire population — already homogenous — became even more homogenous. But it didn't stop there. You would only *feed* on a certain class of people, too. And so the Agent (what your friend Walter calls 'V'), began to concentrate in certain bloodlines while it waned in others. You were not doing your job as a species. You were not spreading the spark of vampirism — which, ironically, doubles as the spark of humanity." He turned his head and stared over with his sharp blue eyes. "But, you see, Reginald — blood needs to circulate. It is not enough for it to simply exist as blood."

"Mmm," said Reginald. "That's poetic. But I still don't think I can let you off the hook for all the human deaths."

The angel finished his drink, looked at the can with reverence, then set it aside. "*We* didn't kill them," he said.

"For inciting those deaths by frightening a race of murderers, then. The slaughter happened in your name. 'For the angels,' and all that. Timken told me that himself. He didn't even want to do it. He said that he liked humans, but was convinced that this was the only way. Of course, he was a psychopath, but that was his reason in the end: because you'd led him to believe that there was no other way."

"There *was* no other way."

Reginald shook his head, then turned his torso toward the angel and put an over-the-top quizzical expression on his face. "Tell me, sage," he said. "How is that, exactly?"

Balestro stood. He looked down at Reginald, who remained seated.

"Humans are your natural predators," he said. "If they couldn't stir your population enough to break the bottleneck, what could? I would have thought you'd have seen that in your bloodline. That's one of the main reasons I gave you the ability to see the bloodline, you know."

"I thought vampires were the predators."

Balestro laughed. "Vampires would think that."

The angel took a step back, then seemed to pose.

"Are you leaving?" said Reginald.

"I'm standing."

"It looks like you're getting ready to vanish or something. Like you're about to leave."

The angel nodded toward the side of the porch. "I figured I'd just walk back the way I came," he said. But then, instead of moving, he stood as if waiting for Reginald to speak — as if he felt Reginald had something to ask and wanted to give him the opportunity.

"Okay," said Reginald. "I have to ask. Why me?"

"Why you *what?*"

But Reginald wasn't sure. Why had he been turned in the first place? Why did he have to be the one to show Lafontaine the light? Why had he been the one to solve the codex? There were too many questions.

"You were in the right place at the right time," the angel continued when he realized Reginald wasn't going to speak. Then he added, "... fatass."

Reginald started to get to his feet, annoyed. But then he saw that the angel was smiling.

THE BLUSH on the horizon was much brighter when Nikki walked out of the house and sat where Balestro had been sitting. Mere reds had given way to oranges that painted the entire eastern sky the dull color of sherbet. She hooked her arm through his, then leaned her head on his shoulder.

"This is going to be the most romantic burning alive ever," she said, looking at the horizon.

"Did you know," said Reginald, "that it turns out that diversity is important enough to die for? That it is, in fact, important enough to exterminate an entire planet for?"

Nikki asked what Reginald meant. He told her about Balestro's brief visit and, as he'd sat alone for the past few minutes, his own growing certainty that his outsider status had, for once in his 79 years, finally been an asset.

"An asset."

"Yes. Mix up the gene pool. Mix up those who the vampires feed on. Mix up the humans by killing most of them, forcing their hardest, most resourceful traits to rise to the surface. Then mix up the vampires with a hard reset — a paradigm shift of epic proportions."

"So you're anticipating more misfit vampires in the future."

"That, yes. But I was also thinking about Lafontaine. Do you think he would have been as willing to listen to a thin, muscle-bound, stunningly attractive vampire as he was to me? Or do you think the message sounded better coming from an imperfect messenger — someone who, thanks to some heft around the middle, reminded him of himself?"

Nikki moved her arm to hug him more fully. She couldn't get her arms around him. She'd never be able to. Never, never, never. And finally, for once, that seemed okay.

"Maybe he saw your emotion. Your compassion. Your emotional flaws."

"I have flaws?"

"Many of them," she said.

They had a few minutes left before the sun rose. Neither was in a rush to start the first of several very long days, operating for at least a while on the humans' schedule. Reginald had already blanked humanity's collective memories through the connection Claire's turning had made possible — all but Lafontaine and a few dozen hand-picked strategists, anyway — and today millions of people would wake up and invent their own stories for their current situations that didn't involve vampires. Those stories, although thought up by millions of individual minds, would form a strangely coherent tapestry — almost as if the whole big lie had been coordinated through blood.

Nikki reached up and unbuttoned the top button on her shirt. Reginald rolled up his cuffs. But still they sat, both wanting to wait as long as they could to go inside.

The pre-sunrise dawn was too beautiful to leave. It felt like the first sunrise the world had ever seen. And in a way, it was.

"So are you going to do it? Take over the presidency?"

"I don't want to be president."

"You can't be thinking of letting Walker do it."

"No way. Besides, he's busy. He's off having as much sex as possible. He found a group of sorority girls who were all turned at once, but who are still giggly."

"Who will lead, then?" Nikki asked.

"Why is that my problem?"

"Because you're the Chosen One."

He shook his head. "Not anymore. Now I'm just really, really, *reeeeeally* smart. And also someone you wouldn't want to play in Trivial Pursuit." Then, when Nikki didn't stop staring at him, he said, "I was thinking maybe Brian could do it."

Nikki nodded. The entire Vampire Nation, now that VNN had suddenly and inexplicably become pro-Reginald, was already starting to look to the former misfit for direction. The world's vampires had been beaten up pretty badly, and it would take some convincing to not lose their collective cool and strike back at the now-glamoured humans. But the blood farms had been liberated, and the truth — for every vampire alive — was that they would need to start learning to hunt, feed, and then make the humans forget that they existed. There would be plenty of hiccups along the way, and someone needed to call the shots. Brian was used to politics, and Reginald was used to being an advisor. It would work out somehow.

"Was that it with the angel, then?" said Nikki after they'd sat in silence for a while. "He just told you that the Ring of Fire was a farce, but that you'd done well as a Chosen One?"

"He also called me a fatass."

"What an asshole." She kept her cheek against his chest, enjoying the moment. It was getting warm. Reginald couldn't speak for Nikki, but the moment was perfect enough that he was almost willing to risk burns to keep it from ending.

"I think he was suggesting that I claim the title, seeing as people are going to say and think it anyway. Like how gay people claimed 'queer' and took away its sting."

"Interesting. Who knew angels were so morally responsible?"

"Maurice calls me 'fatass' too," he said.

Nikki pulled her head away from Reginald's chest and looked into his face. His use of the present tense had thrown her. *"Calls?"*

"In my blood." He tapped his head. "In here."

"Oh."

"But I did ask Balestro about that, after he insulted me. I said, 'The memories you let me see, in my blood — are they just memories? Or are they something more?' But he didn't answer with an answer. He answered with a question."

"What was the question?"

"He said, 'What's the difference?'"

Nikki looked like she was about to respond, but instead she laid her head back on Reginald's shoulder.

Sometime later, they started to blister, so they walked inside. They pulled the shutters, sealed the cracks, and turned on the lights. The world became as it had always been: four walls and two people. Inside, with the shutters drawn, today could be yesterday, could be the day before. The rebellion could be in full swing, the war could be on, or they could be back in Reginald's old house in Columbus, waiting for the day to end and another night shift to begin. Back when Nikki was human. Back when Claire was just a little girl.

"You've got a call with Lafontaine in two hours. So what now?" said Nikki. "Should we sleep?"

Reginald shook his head.

"Should we check to see if Fangbook is still up?"

Again, Reginald shook his head.

She looked at him, a playful expression on her face. "What should we do, then?"

Reginald took her hand. His blood ran in her veins and her blood ran in his. They were two halves of the same whole, and below the top layer of consciousness, they were barely distinguishable. She blinked, and he saw the blink in his own eyes. Then he blinked, and watched as she jumped, having seen it in hers. Then he closed his eyes as they eased onto the couch, both of them becoming more mind than being, more blood than body.

As the room faded and the internal world began to surround them, he said, "Let's go for a walk together, and see who we can find along the way."

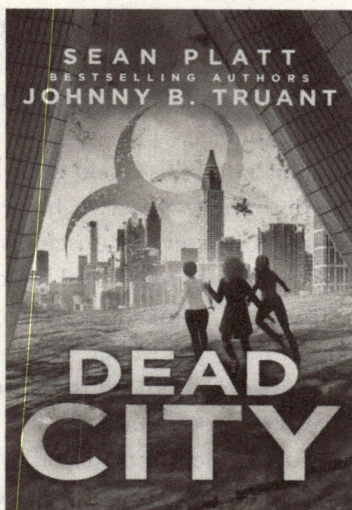

If you loved the *Fat Vampire* series, they you'll definitely want to check out the Platt & Truant take on Zombies. Get *Dead City* and start the *Dead World Trilogy* today!

Get Dead City Today

A Note from the Author

Thanks for reading *Fat Vampire 6: Survival of the Fattest.*

If you enjoyed reading it please leave a review on your favorite bookselling site so others can enjoy it too. Just a couple of sentences would mean a lot to me.

Thank you!

Johnny B Truant

Also by Johnny B Truant

The Fat Vampire Series

Fat Vampire

Fat Vampire 2: Tastes Like Chicken

Fat Vampire 3: All You Can Eat

Fat Vampire 4: Harder, Better, Fatter, Stronger

Fat Vampire 5: Fatpocaplypse

Fat Vampire 6: Survival of the Fattest

The Fat Vampire Chronicles

The Vampire Maurice

Anarchy and Blood

Vampires in the White City

Fangs and Fame

About the Author

Johnny B. Truant is co-owner of the Sterling & Stone Story Studio, an IP powerhouse focusing on books and adaptations for film and television. It's the best job in the world, and he spends his days creating cool stuff with partners Sean Platt and David W. Wright, as well as more than 20 gifted storytellers.

Johnny is the bestselling author of over 100 books under various pen names, including the Fat Vampire and Invasion series. On the nonfiction side, he's also co-author of the indie publishing mainstay Write. Publish. Repeat. and co-host of the weekly Story Studio Podcast.

Originally from Ohio, Johnny and his family now live in Austin, Texas, where he's finally surrounded by creative types as weird as he is.

CPSIA information can be obtained
at www.ICGtesting.com
Printed in the USA
BVHW042218220123
656884BV00027B/478

9 781629 551364